MANTRAS & MINOTAURS

LEVIATHAN FITNESS #3

ASHLEY BENNETT

Illustrated by
CONKY

BEIGNET PUBLISHING

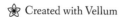

Romance readers over thirty, this one's for you.

CONTENT

This book includes the following: mentions of spousal death, discussion of menopause related body changes, THC use, alcohol consumption, nonhuman love interest, toy play, praise, light spanking, light exhibitionism, "shoving it back in."

PLAYLIST

MANTRAS & MINOTAURS

"American Girl" - Tom Petty and the Heartbreakers
"You Can Call Me Al" - Paul Simon
"When It's Over"- Sugar Ray
"Hey, Hey, What Can I Do" - Led Zeppelin
"Hand In My Pocket" - Alan's Morissette
"Say Hello, Wave Goodbye" - Soft Cell
"Daughter" - Pearl Jam
"Shake the Frost (Live)" - Tyler Childers
"Dreams" - The Cranberries
"Here's Where the Story Ends" - The Sundays
"Halah" - Mazzy Star
"If It Makes You Happy" - Sheryl Crow
"Fast Car" - Tracy Chapman
"Mary Jane's Last Dance" - Tom Petty and the
Heartbreakers
"Night Moves" - Bob Sager
"Losing a Whole Year" - Third Eye Blind
"Going to California" - Led Zeppelin
"There She Goes" - The La's

"All Apologies (Live MTV Unplugged)" - Nirvana
"Here Comes My Girl" - Tom Petty and the Heartbreakers

ONE

PAM

January 1st

Look back at the past, marvel at how far you have come.

Winding down for the evening, I sipped my boxed wine, letting out a deep sigh as Harry kissed Sally in what was probably one of the most romantic cinematic kisses of all time. I mean, Billy Crystal definitely didn't do it for me, but Meg Ryan—that was a totally different story.

The holiday season had come and gone here in Briar Glenn, and I'd spent last night, New Year's Eve, alone at home watching romance movies with my cat.

Since the loss of my husband, Don, two years ago, a certain hairless gentleman had become my constant companion. My son Reece swore that Remi was some sort of alien, but the cat rescue assured me that he was a Sphynx.

'You know, Remi," I said to him, lifting the blanket he was sleeping under so he would have to acknowledge me. "That right there is true love. When you meet someone and you just know."

My daughter Tegan and her fated mate came to mind. She'd called me raving about the buff wolven the same day he'd helped her scrape wedding cake off the pavement outside my bakery. *Well, it was her bakery now.*

When Don passed, he left me a sizable pension, more than enough to be comfortable, and I was happy to pass on my business to Tegan. She'd been helping out at the bakery since she was a little girl. Truth be told, she was probably glad I was out of her hair.

I'd been feeling like that a lot lately.

Both of my children had their own lives. They'd been drawn to their fated mates by the goddess. Atlas and Tegan were engaged to be married, and Reece and Cyrus were, well, they were new puppy parents.

Everyone else around me was thriving. Living. But it felt like I was stuck in the same place, watching as life passed me by.

Don't get me wrong, I had my hobbies: reading, knitting Remi and myself matching sweaters, and volunteering at the library two days a week.

But there was still a void.

Yes, Don was gone, but his passing hadn't impacted me the way I expected it would. He was my high school sweetheart and we married young, just like lots of folks in small towns do. Before I knew it, I was pregnant with Reece, and Tegan followed soon after.

Don wasn't the best partner or father, but when you

have kids and a life that is so utterly interconnected, especially in a small town, you're just sort of...*stuck*.

There were good moments, but they were outweighed by disagreements and nights spent with the kids at my mother's house.

Seeing my children in such healthy, happy relationships made me elated, but every once in a while, jealousy crept in.

This was one of those times.

I grabbed my phone, scrolling my social media feed absentmindedly before pulling up my messages.

I typed out a quick text to Tegan, just like I did anytime I was bored.

> Me: Hi, honey. I hope you and Atlas had a great New Year's. Are you up for a chat?

My phone rang a few moments later.

"Hey, Mom! What's up?" Tegan sounded awfully upbeat for it being New Year's Day, but then again she didn't really drink. Neither of my kids did. It made me proud but it also made me question if Don and I were the reason why.

Without thinking too hard about it, I took another sip of my wine before answering. "Just sitting at home with Remi. Did you and Atlas have a good New Year's?"

She let out a deep sigh. "It was okay, I guess. We went over to Javier's house. Him and Fallon got drunk and wrestled in the front yard. Atlas had to break it up."

Javier was so sweet; I had a hard time believing it. "Are you serious? Is everyone okay?"

"Yeah. Atlas managed to calm both of them down and everyone was fine by the time the ball dropped—but it was still a stupid display of masculinity."

"Were your brother and Cyrus there?" I was positive

the answer would be yes. Reece and Tegan had worked to repair their relationship the past few months and more often than not, they could be found hanging out together with their mates.

It helped that Atlas and Cyrus were best friends too.

"Of course they were. They left before the fight happened though. Reece said they had to go home to check on Beau. He is such a worrywart when it comes to that puppy," Tegan teased with a laugh.

"I still can't believe Cyrus surprised him like that. He is such a gem." I had all but given up on Reece finding a partner, but when he'd started training for the triathlon with Cyrus, it was obvious they had more than just a coach/trainee relationship.

"Yeah, he is. I'm still not sure Mr. Grumpy Pants deserves him though."

I was mid-sip when she said that, my snort almost sending my wine out of my nose and all over my white, knit blanket.

Her lighthearted giggle echoed through the phone. "What about you, Mom? Did you do anything fun last night?"

I answered as soon as the burning sensation in my sinuses subsided. "Well, I drank wine, watched romance movies on the couch with Remi, and worked on a new set of matching sweaters." Gods, it sounded so depressing when I rehashed it aloud like that.

"Mom..." Tegan's voice was heavy with concern, or maybe pity. "I really wish you'd get out more."

"I'd love to, but it's hard to meet new people when you live in a town like Briar Glenn."

"You know, there's this dating app Javier uses—"

I cut her off. "Don't you think I'm a little too old for a

dating app?" I thought they were something used by young people to find hookups, not fifty-four-year-old women seeking companionship with the potential for romance.

Tegan snorted, which brought a smile to my face. "Mom, you're not old. I really think you should download it and make a profile. If you don't like it, you can just delete the app and it'll be like it never happened."

I did want to see who was out there...

"Fine. I'll check it out. What's it called?" I transferred her to speakerphone so I could search for it.

"It's called Mate Match. It only allows profiles to message you if you've already marked them as a match you'd be interested in."

Huh. Well, it sounded like there was a certain level of safety and anti-harassment built into the app. "Alright, I'm downloading it now."

Tegan squealed and I jumped, almost spilling my wine.

"You have to tell me if you match with anyone. Promise me you'll tell me?" she pleaded.

"I promise, but I doubt I'm going to match with anyone."

"Mom. Seriously? You're a babe. Besides, some younger men are into older women."

I tsked. "Oh no, no, no. No younger men for me. They need to be my age or older—no exceptions."

"Make sure you set your age preferences on the app then. Let me know if I need to come over tomorrow and help you with it, okay?"

I knew she was trying to be helpful, but I wasn't so old that I couldn't figure out how to set up my own profile on a dating app. How hard could it be?

"Will do, honey. Give Atlas my love."

"I will. And remember to text me if you match. I'm serious, Mom. I want to see pictures!"

"Pinky promise. Bye sweetie."

I hung up the phone before she could get another word in.

Tegan seemed confident I'd find a match, but I wasn't so sure.

I peered down at my phone through my bifocals, the blue light reflecting off my lenses as I scrolled through my photo gallery, searching for a profile pic.

There were limited options. Me with Remi. Me with Reece and Tegan. Me with Atlas.

I didn't want to give the impression that I was already taken or that my kids were my entire personality. I mean, they were, but that wasn't the sort of information I wanted to advertise right out of the gate.

Eventually, I stumbled upon a picture Tegan had snapped of me last Christmas. I was wearing a rust-colored sweater I'd knit myself, a black skirt, and a pair of pumps that matched my sweater. My ruby red hair was streaked with gray and piled high on top of my head in a messy bun, my freshly cut bangs just barely touching the rim of my glasses. Even though the photo was a year old, it was recent enough that I still looked the same. And in the words of my daughter, *like a total babe.*

"Let's see here," I mumbled to myself as I uploaded my profile picture and scanned the categories.

Employment.

Well, I was retired, which was fairly uncommon at my age, but I supposed it was best not to lie about it.

Education.

That one stung. I always wanted to go to college, but between Don and the kids, it wasn't in the cards for me.

Let's just go with 'some college'. Surely, the pottery class I took at the local community college counted as *something*.

Location.

Briar Glenn, of course. I was well aware of who was available to date here, so I selected a radius that would include the three neighboring towns.

About me.

Hmm.

Do you include that you're widowed in your profile? What kind of vibe does that give off? What if they think I'm some sort of black widow, meeting males on dating apps and murdering them once my name is listed as the beneficiary on their insurance policy?

Gods, I'd been listening to way too many true crime podcasts.

I tapped a manicured nail against the glass of my phone, pondering what else to say about myself. This was always so difficult.

Ultimately, I decided to go with:

Widowed. Knitter. Avid reader of romance books. Film buff. Former wedding cake baker and pastry shop owner. Mom to two amazing adult children (and one hairless cat). Looking for companionship with the potential for something more.

Sweet and concise.

Just like me.

Remi ambled back in from the kitchen and jumped on my lap as I set the age range for acceptable matches.

"What do you think, Rem? Should I open it up to younger men? Is sixty too old? I mean forty is the new thirty, so fifty must be the new forty, making sixty the new fifty. I'm fifty-four, so it's only a six-year age difference."

The tiny, wrinkled gremlin stared up at me, his wide eyes unblinking.

"Alright, sixty it is."

Was I really one of those people who stayed at home and asked their cat rhetorical questions?

The answer was yes, yes I was.

Once I'd set the parameters for appropriate matches, I watched eagerly as a loading bar flashed across the screen. This was the part I was most excited about. I'd heard about the swiping and I was anxious to experience it for myself.

The first profile suggested for me was a human man in his late forties. He was cute, but according to his bio, he was in an open relationship.

I admired folks who could do open relationships, but it wasn't my style. Even though I was looking for something casual, I wasn't too keen on sharing a partner. Apparently, all those years of monogamy had really done a number on me.

Photo after photo passed on the screen as I swiped left on pretty much every profile. Humans, monsters—none of them drew me in.

Until a candid shot of a curly-haired minotaur caught my attention.

His hair was a light cream color, full of cowlicks that curled in all different directions. A set of ridged, deep brown horns curled overtop of his head, running across his fluffy eyebrows and connecting above his snout. His dusty pink nose was adorned with a shiny gold ring, the type you'd commonly see on a bull. A buffalo plaid shirt stretched across his wide chest, with a tuft of hair sprinkled with grays sticking out from beneath the unbuttoned collar.

Gods, he was handsome.

Another photo showed him standing on a rocky mountainside with a backpack strapped to his back, a wide grin plastered to his face as he gave the camera a thumbs up. It appeared he was quite the outdoorsman.

The third photo showed him sipping from a tiny espresso cup with his pinky out in a display of civility.

So he was a caffeine guy.

Now that I could get behind.

According to his profile, his name was Alistair.

Alistair.

How distinguished.

He was a fifty-five-year-old divorcé who worked in the agricultural industry. A suspicious maple leaf graced that portion of his profile...Did that mean he worked in the marijuana industry?

Although I'd embraced the whole grunge aesthetic in the '90s, I'd never smoked pot before...How would that even work?

I mean, not everyone who worked in that industry smoked pot, right? There was no way the investors with their tailored suits were toking doobies in their high rises.

I was being ridiculous. Weed was legal in some states. I was making a stink about nothing.

His location was listed as...right here in Briar Glenn?

He must have moved here recently. I would have seen him around town, I'm sure of it.

I scrolled to his About Me.

I live in Colorado, but I'm visiting to help care for my daughter. I have a degree in agriculture and work in the cannabis industry. I enjoy the great outdoors, coffee, and good food with even better

company. I'm looking for casual, no strings attached
fun.

Well, it appeared I should edit my profile. His was
much more professional.

My finger hovered over his photo.

He was visiting from another state, but I wasn't looking
for anything serious. Maybe I was getting ahead of myself...

"Aw, what the hell," I said to Remi, and swiped right.

Now to wait and see if he'd respond.

TWO

ALISTAIR

What you seek is seeking you, too.

"Chai, hun. You alright in there?" I asked as I rapped my knuckles on the bathroom door.

"I'm fine, Dad. Can't I use the bathroom in peace?" she groaned from behind the door.

"Sorry, sorry. My bad. Just wanted to make sure you were all good." I heard her let out a deep sigh as I walked down the hall toward the guest room I was staying in.

My daughter, Chai, had been dealing with some health issues, and I'd flown in from Colorado to take care of her. With my position as the CEO of a cannabis cultivation and distribution company, I was able to work remotely and provide her with the support she needed to get better.

And better she was. We'd spent the holidays together for the first time in who knew how long, and I could tell my presence was wearing on her patience.

Sure, we were close, but we hadn't lived together for

quite some time. She was a grown minotaur who was used to her independence and privacy. I interfered with that.

I'd be out of her hair soon enough, though. Now that she was well, I was scheduled to fly back to Colorado in two days' time. While part of me was anxious to get back to the mountains, I didn't have anything waiting for me back home besides work.

Chai's mother and I had divorced when she was young, and I'd put my kid and work first, prioritizing those two things above all else. I was a great father, and damn successful, but I wished I had someone to share that success with. My life was lonely. As hard as it was to admit, it was the truth. I was ready to find someone to share my golden years with.

So, at Chai's urging, I'd joined some dating apps. I'd had a few dates here and there, but I never felt that strong connection I was looking for.

I threw myself onto the guest bed I'd called my own for the past month and pulled out my phone for some good old-fashioned doom scrolling. Thankfully, I had Chai to keep me hip on all the lingo kids were using these days.

A notification popped up on the screen from Mate Match.

I had a match.

Vibrant red hair and bright green eyes framed by thick-rimmed glasses caught my attention.

Pam was fifty-four years old, a retired widow, who enjoyed knitting, film, and reading.

There was no way this woman was fifty-four. She didn't look a day over forty.

While in Briar Glenn this past month, the app had been dead silent. So, of course, a few days before I was scheduled to leave, I'd get a match.

My finger hovered over the message button. Her profile said she was looking for something casual, and who knew if she'd even be available to grab a coffee or something before I left town?

At first glance, it didn't seem like we had much in common, but there were only so many things you could cram into a short bio. I was sure we could find something to talk about. Plus, she was drop-dead gorgeous.

What the hell.

I tapped the message button.

Shit.

What should I say? I saw your profile and thought you looked hot? That sounded like something a teenage boy would say—not a grown male.

Maybe just a simple hello, how are you doing?

That was good right? A casual conversation starter.

> Me: Hey there! How are you doing?

I pressed send and stared at my phone, waiting for her to respond. We'd just matched, so she had to have her phone nearby. My phone buzzed with an incoming message.

It was her.

> Pam: Hi! I'm well, thanks. How are you?

How was I doing?

Well, I was over the moon that she'd responded, but it wasn't exactly like I could say that.

> Me: I'm doing great. I stumbled upon your profile and thought I'd say hello. It looks like you're new here on the app?

Another instant response.

> Pam: I am! My husband passed away a few years ago and I decided it's finally time to put myself out there. I'm just looking for something casual though. Nothing too serious, at least not right away.

We were sort of in the same boat then. Besides, I wouldn't be in town long enough for it to develop into something serious. But a relaxed coffee date with an attractive woman? That I could do.

> Me: It may be sort of forward of me to ask, but would you want to meet for coffee? Tomorrow? I'm leaving Briar Glenn in a few days to head back to my home in Colorado.

I figured that would be the killing blow, the fact that in a few days' time I'd be back at my cabin in the Rockies. I didn't expect a reply, assuming she'd ghost me, but to my surprise, she messaged me back.

> Pam: You're only here for a few more days and you'd like to spend some of that time with me?

> Me: Yes, is that weird?

Did she think I was some creep?

Pam: Not at all. I'd love to get coffee with you.

Me: It's a date then. Tomorrow at 9 a.m., the coffee shop on 5th and Main?

Pam: I'll see you then.

Me: Looking forward to it! :)

I couldn't stop the wide smile that stretched across my face.

"Why are you smiling at your phone like an idiot?" Chai leaned against the doorway, assessing me like only a daughter could.

"I'm smiling at my phone like an idiot because I just asked a woman to go on a date with me tomorrow," I said proudly.

"No way! Your last day here and you're going to spend it doing something other than playing Candy Smash!" she shrieked and plopped down beside me on the bed, her hands reaching for my phone. "Who? Let me see her!"

Chai squealed when I handed her my phone. "Dad. Do you know who this is?"

I shook my head no.

"This is Tegan's mom! You know, Atlas from the gym? His mate's mom!"

I'd met Atlas a few times when he'd stopped by to check on Chai, but I'd never met his mate. "Oh, yeah? What's their family like?"

She stood and handed me my phone. "Well, I've never met her mom, but Tegan is super sweet. She owns the bakery on Main Street."

So that's what she meant by former bakery owner. Her

daughter had taken over her business. I loved that, and in this day and age, it wasn't all that common.

"So I guess it's out of the question to suggest we go there after we get coffee?" I was clueless when it came to dating, even more so in a town that wasn't my own. I needed Chai's help.

"You should take her ice skating at the rink they put up in the park. It's romantic. What about the rest of her profile? What does it say she likes?"

"Uhh..." I squinted down at the tiny screen. I needed readers, but I was holding out as long as I could. "It says she likes knitting, romance books, and movies."

Chai tapped her hoof on the floor, her tail swishing back and forth behind her. "The movies are a no-go for a first date—not conducive to conversation. Stick with the coffee shop, treat her to a book at the bookstore, and then if you're hitting it off, suggest ice skating."

I smiled at my daughter. "You know, for someone who refuses to date, you're pretty good at this, kid. You should follow your own advice sometime."

She shook her head. "I'm good, thanks."

"Chai, you can't let—"

Her eyes about rolled out of her head. "Anywayyy, are you sure this is a good idea right before you leave? What if you really hit it off with Pam?"

I shrugged. "We both said we're looking for something casual. It's just one date."

"Mhmm." Chai crossed her arms over her chest. "Don't make her catch feelings and then break her heart. Her soon-to-be son-in-law is my boss."

She was being ridiculous. I hadn't been in a relationship for years. Why would this be any different? "One date,

Chai. Coffee, the bookstore, and maybe some ice skating. It's one date."

"Whatever you say." She turned her back to me and started off down the hall. "Sleep tight, Romeo," she called out.

"Night, kid," I grumbled.

Sometimes adult children were more of a pain in the ass than they were as kids.

I rose from the bed with a groan and shut the door. Slipping off my clothes, I changed into my sweatpants, threading my tail through the hole in the back. I turned off the light and climbed back into bed.

For a good fifteen minutes, I tossed and turned. No matter how much I tried to relax, sleep just wouldn't find me. It was a shame I didn't bring any edibles with me. Those always did the trick.

My phone vibrated from where I'd set it on the nightstand.

A Mate Match message from Pam.

I unlocked my phone, the bright light irritating my eyes in the otherwise dark room.

Pam: Are you awake??

Huh. It seemed someone else was having a hard time sleeping.

Me: I'm up. Is everything okay?

Ugh. I hoped she wasn't about to cancel on me. This was the first thing I'd looked forward to in I don't know how long.

> Pam: I'm just having a hard time falling asleep. I think I'm nervous about tomorrow.

She was nervous about our date. It was fucking cute. I mean, I was nervous too. Might as well admit it.

> Me: I'm nervous too.

> Pam: Would you want to chat on the phone for a bit? I know it's old school, but it might help ease our nerves a little.

It was old school. In the age of text messaging, I rarely talked on the phone anymore. A random phone call or video chat with Chai was pretty much it. Getting to know one another before meeting would be nice though...

> Me: Sure. My number is 398-459-3745.

My phone vibrated with an incoming call from an unknown number a few moments later.

"Hey." My voice sounded gruff so I cleared my throat. "Pam?"

"Alistair?" Her voice was smooth and pleasant, just like I thought she'd sound.

"The one and only," I said with a laugh and she followed suit. Within the first minute of our call, I'd already made her laugh. I'd call that a win.

"Thank you for doing this. I'm just so nervous. I didn't expect to match so soon, let alone set up a date. I literally signed up for the app today."

That explained why we'd just matched. "Your first day on the app and my ugly mug gets a right swipe from you—and a date! It must be my lucky day."

Another warm, lighthearted laugh. "You did not just call yourself ugly."

I mean, yeah, I was handsome. But when you compared me to someone like her? She was way out of my league. "I mean, if the shoe fits—"

"I happen to think you're quite handsome. Unless your pictures are photoshopped or they're old." There was a hint of a smile in her voice.

I chuckled. "I can assure you, they're definitely not photoshopped or filtered or anything like that. The one of me on the cliffside is from last year, but the rest my daughter took when she visited me a few months ago."

"What's your daughter's name?"

"Chai. I found out that she knows your daughter and works for your soon-to-be son-in-law."

"Get out of town. She works at Leviathan Fitness?" Pam asked.

"Mhmm. Well, when she isn't on medical leave."

"Oh no. I'm so sorry to hear that."

"It's alright. She's doing much better now. That's actually why I'm heading back to Colorado. I stayed with her for a month while she recovered." For dramatic effect, and to lighten the mood, I lowered my voice. "I think she can't wait for me to leave."

Pam broke out into laughter, making me grin. "I can only imagine if I had to stay with either of my kids for a month. They'd be the same way."

"You have two?"

"Yes. My son, Reece, is thirty-five and my daughter, Tegan, is thirty."

My mouth hung open. "You have a thirty-five-year-old?"

She laughed again. "Don't sound so surprised! I started early! How old is your daughter?"

"She's twenty-five. I was thirty when she was born. Her mom and I divorced a few years later."

My ex-wife and I had our fair share of problems. Rather than continue on in a loveless marriage full of arguments, we decided to go our separate ways. It was a lot healthier for us to co-parent Chai instead of dragging out our relationship. Custody was split evenly between the two of us, so I never felt like I missed out on Chai's childhood.

Pam hummed in understanding. "Sometimes that's for the best. My husband and I almost got to that point a few times, but we stuck it out for Reece and Tegan. I'm not sure it was the right thing to do, but the past is the past. There's nothing I can do about it now."

That's right. She was a widow. Should I bring up her husband?

An awkward silence stretched between us before Pam finally spoke again. "Most people don't know what to say when you lose your spouse. It's been a little over two years since Don passed, and honestly, my life is a lot better without him."

"It sounds like we were in similar situations."

She sighed. "But you were smart enough to walk away."

I didn't like hearing her put herself down. "Hey. None of that. Relationships are complex, especially when there are kids involved. You did what you thought was best for them. It sounds like you're a great mom."

"I'd like to think so." The so was stretched out by a yawn.

I smiled to myself. If she was this sweet in person, I was going to be in trouble. "I should probably get to bed. It's getting late and I have a hot date in the morning."

"That's funny," she murmured. "I have a hot date, too."

"Well make sure you tell him how lucky he is to be out with you."

"Will do. Goodnight, Alistair."

"Goodnight, Pam."

I hung up the phone and stared at the dark ceiling while thoughts of Pam Rollins swirled around in my head. I already suspected one coffee date might not be enough.

THREE

PAM

"The art of living happily is to live in the present." -
Pythagoras

After Alistair and I hung up last night, I still struggled to fall
asleep, staying up into the early morning hours.

He was just so dang charming.

Not to mention how easy it was to have a conversation
with him.

He'd also made me laugh a time or two. A sense of
humor was always something I'd admired in a partner, but it
was something Don never had. In all our years together, I
could probably count the number of times he'd made me
laugh on one hand. And when he did make me laugh, it was
at the expense of our children or other people. He just—
hadn't been a very nice person.

I guess that's why I didn't feel any guilt about my date
with Alistair. Sure, I was nervous, but there was zero guilt
there.

"Good morning," I said to Remi as he emerged from beneath the covers next to me. "Big day today, buddy. Mama's got a date."

He gave me a look of displeasure as if the fact that I wasn't already up and preparing his breakfast personally offended him. To be fair, it probably did.

Cats.

I got out of bed at the behest of my wrinkled overlord, ready to indulge in coffee and contemplation before getting ready for my date. It was only six-thirty, so I had plenty of time to get ready and dwell on the fact that, for the first time in years, I was going on a date.

How early was too early to call Tegan?

I fed Remi and nursed my first cup of coffee while I typed out a text to Tegan.

> Me: Hey. I have a date this morning. Call me when you can.

My phone rang a couple of minutes later.

"Jeez. Someone is up early," I said with a smile.

"Atlas got up early to go for a run, and I've been awake ever since," she groaned.

My daughter was never much of a morning person, but she was mated to one of the most pleasant early risers I'd ever met. Opposites attract and all that, I guess.

"Well, that's a shame, honey."

"Yeah, yeah. Enough about me," she rushed out. "What's this about a date? I thought I told you to text me if you got a match. How did you even get a match already?"

I gasped. "Excuse me. I believe that yesterday someone called me a babe."

"Oh my gosh, stop. You know that isn't what I meant. Tell me everything! Send me pics!"

"Alright, alright." I grabbed my glasses off the table and put Tegan on speakerphone. "His name is Alistair. He's actually your friend's father."

"Which friend?" I could hear the anticipation in her voice.

"Chai?"

She let out a screeching sound that reminded me of a dying animal. "No way. You're going on a date with Chai's dad? Did you send me that picture yet?"

"I'm working on it!"

I gulped down some coffee and navigated to Alistair's profile, screenshotting the picture of him on the mountainside and sending it over to her.

"Sent."

I could hear her phone buzz with a notification.

"Damn, Mom! He is a hottie. Those horns and that chest hair."

My lips curved up in a smile. "I think he is too."

Tegan let out another little squeal. "This is amazing. Since it's Chai's dad, I don't have to worry about him being some sort of creep."

"He definitely doesn't seem like a creep. We talked on the phone for a little bit last night. We—"

She cut me off. "You talked to him on the phone last night?! Who are you and what have you done with my mother?"

"We were both nervous about today!" I said with a laugh. "It doesn't sound like he does much dating."

"Well, it sounds like you made a good impression. What time are you meeting him?"

"I'm meeting him at the coffee shop down the street from the bakery at nine."

"Aww," she said with a dreamy sigh. "That's a perfect first date."

"I think so. It's casual, though. He goes back to Colorado tomorrow."

"Like, for a trip?"

"No, honey. He lives there. He was only here to look after Chai while she was sick."

"Mom." She sounded apprehensive. It was like our roles had reversed, with her as the mother and me as the child. "Are you sure this is a good idea? I don't want you to get hurt."

"There's nothing to worry about. It's not like I'm going to fall in love with him after one date."

I'd been trapped in a loveless marriage and spent the last two years alone. I was no stranger to it being me, myself, and I. Well, *and Remi*.

"I just worry, that's all. You've been through a lot over the past few years. I want you to meet someone, but I want it to be someone who's going to stick around."

She was sweet.

"It's just coffee and conversation. One date, then we'll go our separate ways."

"Okay...What are you going to wear?"

Oh, she was definitely my daughter, changing the topic like that. It was a real Pam Rollins move, but I'd cut her a break and go with it.

"I was thinking about wearing a sweater, leggings, boots, and that nice coat you got for me."

"That'll be really cute. Send me pics before you head out, and promise you'll call me as soon as you get home. I don't anticipate Chai's dad being a serial killer, but you never know."

"That thought never even crossed my mind. Love you, honey."

"Love you, too, Mom. Have fun!"

We hung up, and I drained what was left of my coffee. I was glad Tegan shared in my excitement, and in a way, I was relieved that she didn't bring up her father or ask if I was feeling any guilt over going on a date. Reece had always been fairly detached from Don, but Tegan was a total daddy's girl. Growing up, he'd treated them both differently, which always rubbed me the wrong way.

Whenever I tried to bring it up, I was told that it was "just how you raised boys." Knowing what I know now, that was so wrong, and it did lasting damage that Reece was just now getting therapy for.

For a second, I contemplated how different things might have been if I'd had the courage to leave, but it passed quickly.

You can't live in the past, only do what you can to improve upon the future.

I was determined to do just that.

I FLUFFED my hair in the mirror, doing a little turn to check my outfit.

I looked good, but I wondered if leggings were too much of a millennial fashion trend for a woman my age. If Tegan had concerns, she would have mentioned them.

Choosing a sweater had proven to be the most difficult part of getting ready. As an avid knitter, I had quite the collection. But ultimately, I'd decided to go with the rust-colored sweater from my dating profile picture. Yeah, it was a little weird, and maybe he'd think I didn't own other clothing, but it complemented my hair and eye color.

Remi jumped onto the bathroom counter and rubbed his hairless face against my hip.

"How do I look, bud?" I asked my kitty companion.

I pulled out my phone, snapped a few pictures of us, and sent them to Tegan.

Tegan: Hot mama! Have a great time!!

Shit.

The timestamp on the message read eight forty-five. I lived right down the street from the coffee shop, planning to walk and not worry about parking, but with the ice and snow on the sidewalks, I was cutting it close.

"Alright, little man. I've gotta get going. Wish me luck." I gave him an affectionate pat on the back before bustling out of the bathroom and heading downstairs.

Throwing on my coat, I wrapped my favorite knit scarf around my neck. I'd had it since Reece and Tegan were young; it was a gorgeous sage-colored yarn knit in a herringbone pattern.

The cold air stung my nose the second I stepped onto my front porch. I almost regretted walking, but the warmth of the morning sun on my cheeks made me change my mind.

Briar Glenn was such a beautiful town. While it had seen its fair share of growth over the past few years, all the changes had improved it. With the monster integration, the town had undergone a sort of cultural renaissance. There were new businesses, new faces, and a renewed sense of community.

"Morning, Mrs. Rollins," a familiar voice whistled as I neared my future son-in-law's gym.

I glanced up to find Fallon, Atlas' best friend and Cyrus' former roommate, giving me a friendly flutter of his wing.

"Morning, Fallon! I'd love to chat, but I'm late for my date." I gave him a polite smile and kept walking.

He whistled again as I passed him. "A date?! He's a lucky guy. Have a great time!"

That Fallon sure was a sweetheart, but from what I'd heard from Tegan, he was quite the player when it came to dating.

The sign for the coffee shop came into view and I felt my stomach flip with anxiety.

"It's fine. Everything is going to be fine," I mumbled, walking through the front door.

The rich scent of coffee filled my nose the moment I walked inside. I heard a warm laugh I vaguely recognized, one that brought a smile to my face.

There he was.

Alistair's back was turned to me as he chatted with Brian, the owner and head barista at The Busy Bean.

Holy shit, he was beefy.

And tall, almost as tall as Atlas.

His craggy horns curved toward the ceiling and a worn jacket stretched across his wide back. It was the same one he wore in the mountainside picture, making me feel less awkward about my sweater. Just below the hem of his jacket, his tail stuck out from a hole in his perfectly-fitted jeans and swayed back and forth lazily.

His ears perked up when he heard the overhead bell of the door and he turned to face me.

Sweet heavenly goddess.

He smiled down at me, a soft, lopsided grin full of perfectly white, flat teeth. Long lashes—the type you'd kill for—fanned out over his wide brown eyes. They were deep and expressive, gleaming with excitement and kindness.

He was even more handsome in person.

"Hi there," he said in that gruff voice of his. "You must be Pam."

"Y-yes. H-hi." I needed to get it together. I could barely speak.

He laughed and extended his hefty hand out to me. "I'm Alistair, but you can call me Al."

Al.

He watched me intently as my tongue darted out to wet my lips.

"I take it you're my long-lost pal, then," I said, shaking his hand.

Pam Rollins.

What is wrong with you?

A Paul Simon joke about his name?

Al stared at me for a second before he let out another genuine laugh. "Ha! That's a good one. I love Paul Simon. That entire album is perfection."

The knot in my stomach loosened slightly.

He didn't think it was stupid; he thought it was funny!

"I think it's perfection, too! I hope you haven't been waiting long."

Al ran a hand along his horns, ruffling his cream-colored curls. "Not long at all." He gestured to Brian. "Brian here was just giving me the rundown of their seasonal specialties, and I think I'm all set. Do you know what you'd like to order?"

I peeked around Al, giving Brian a little wave. "The usual please, Brian."

I started digging around in my purse, searching for my wallet, but Al gently grabbed my arm.

"I'd like to treat if that's okay? Have you eaten yet? What about a pastry or something?" He pointed to the blueberry muffins with a crumble top inside the pastry case. "I've been eyeing those muffins."

"Oh, they're to die for."

Al turned to the barista. "And a large Americano and two blueberry muffins please, Brian." He turned back to me and smiled. I couldn't help but beam back up at him. "Why don't you find us a table?"

So. Freaking. Charming.

"Okay," I said with a nod and headed to my favorite table while Al paid for our order.

I took off my scarf and coat, draping them over the back of my chair while I waited for Al.

He was such a gentleman—gentle minotaur? In all my years of marriage, I don't think Don had ever had me take a seat while he grabbed our drinks and food. Sometimes it was the little things that made the biggest impression.

Brian passed Al a tray with our drinks and muffins on it, which he dutifully carried over to me, his hooves clicking along the tile floor as he approached.

"For you, madame," he said, passing me a muffin and my latte.

"Thank you so much."

"It's my pleasure." He sat across from me and took a sip of his Americano. "Ah, sweet caffeine."

I let out a little laugh. The picture of him with the tiny espresso cup made total sense—he was a fellow caffeine fiend.

"I managed to sneak in a cup before I got ready this morning. I needed it," I admitted.

"You look beautiful, by the way."

"Thank you," I said shyly, rubbing my hand over the back of my neck. "You look just as handsome as your pictures."

"Well, thank you. I like your sweater."

I stretched my arms out over the table, showing off one of my favorite pieces of knitwear, and beaming with pride. "Thank you! I made it myself."

"I remember from your profile. I've always been envious of people who can make things."

"It isn't too hard once you get the hang of it."

He snorted, his wide, pink nostrils flaring and the ring between them wiggling slightly. "If we had more time, I'd say that you could teach me."

His words settled like a heavy weight between us. Yes, we'd just met, but I liked him already.

"Mmm," I hummed. "True. Are you excited to go home?"

"Well, I was." He smiled kindly before leaning over the table and whispering, "I'm wishing I had a little more time right about now."

My cheeks heated with a blush.

This was the first time in a long time that I'd felt chemistry like this with someone.

And before I knew it, he'd be returning to Colorado. But that didn't mean we couldn't enjoy it while it lasted.

FOUR

ALISTAIR

"The perfect moment is this one." - Jon Kabat-Zinn

"And the next thing I know, a moose is standing there next to my RV, my underwear hanging from its mouth like it was a dog." A rumbly laugh rolled out of my chest as I told her my favorite camping story.

I'd recounted my funniest stories for the past two hours, trying to make her laugh. She did this adorable little snort thing, and I loved how it sounded.

She fought to catch her breath and dabbed at the corners of her eyes with her napkin. "Oh, gods. That's hilarious. What did you do?"

"Well, I let him keep the underwear, obviously, but I just waited for him to go on his merry way. Moose are dangerous and I didn't want to risk scaring him. That was the last time I hung up my wet clothes in moose territory, though."

She chuckled. "You learned that lesson the hard way."

"I did." I sighed and finished the last of my cold Americano. "I loved the blueberry muffin, by the way. Do you do any baking these days?"

She tilted her head to the side thoughtfully. "You know, not really. I think it's one of things where I spent so long doing it that it's nice to have time away from it. I still bake my kids their birthday cakes every year, though."

She still made their birthday cakes.

With a stupid grin on my face, I stared across the table at Pam. She was beautiful. Funny. Interesting.

How in the world had I been in this little town for a month and not once had I run into her? I mean, our freaking kids were mutual friends.

I was leaving tomorrow and now I was dreading it.

Shit.

It was presumptuous of me, but I felt like we had some real chemistry.

She caught me glancing down at my watch. "Did you have somewhere to be or...?" I could hear the disappointment in her voice.

In reality, I was mentally calculating how much time I had left with this wonderful woman.

"Not at all. I was actually hoping you'd be up for a trip to the bookstore. Maybe some ice skating after that?"

Her face lit up with a bright smile. "I'd love that."

"Good, let's get out of here then." I rose from the table, gathering our cups and plates back onto the tray to return it to Brian.

"Oh, allow me," she said and pushed out of her chair.

"No, no," I insisted. "You get your coat on, and I'll take care of this."

Pam glanced up at me through her glasses. "Alright."

When I returned to the table, she was bundled up with

a green scarf wrapped around her neck, ready to head back out into the January cold.

"I like your scarf," I said as I held the door open for her. "Another one of your knitting creations?"

"Yes," she said, snuggling down into it. "It's ancient, but it's my favorite."

I could see why. It looked well-loved but very cozy.

We headed to the bookstore, walking side by side down the sidewalk, the warmth of the early afternoon sun making the chilly day somewhat tolerable.

Perfect weather for ice skating, I thought to myself.

"Oh gods!" Pam shrieked as she lost her footing, her boots sliding along a patch of ice.

"Whoa there." My hand darted out, grasping Pam's palm tightly as I pulled her to her feet.

"T-thank you," she said as she looked up at me.

Her chest was heaving, her hand still gripping mine.

She felt so small as I stared down at her.

So small, yet so close.

I wanted to lean over and kiss her—but was that too forward? She was a widow, and from the sound of things, her only real experiences had been with her late husband.

Before I could do anything drastic, she made the decision for me, turning her head away and pulling her hand from mine.

A small frown tugged at my lips, but I forced myself to grin instead. It pained me to do it, but this was for the best. I was acting irrationally.

We were silent for the rest of the walk to the bookstore and managed to avoid any more awkward near-kiss incidents.

"Here we are," I said, opening the door for Pam and following her inside.

The Briar Glenn Bookshop was like something out of a magazine. The small store was lined with shelves and tables overflowing with books. It had become one of my favorite places here in town, and I was glad Pam had agreed to accompany me on what would probably be my last visit.

Well, until the next time I visited Chai, that is.

"Hey, Mrs. Rollins!" The petite goth girl behind the counter greeted her with a little wave.

It was charming how everyone knew each other here. I couldn't help but wonder what our date would mean for the town gossip mill, though. In the long run, it wouldn't matter. Tomorrow I'd be on a plane headed back to the Rockies.

Pam loosened her scarf, her eyes already scanning the rows of books in the romance section.

"Romance, eh?" I said with a laugh.

She looked at me and pushed her glasses up her nose. "It's always been my favorite genre. There's comfort in knowing the characters will always get their happy ending."

"Well, I like happy endings." I sidled up beside her, my wide body rubbing against her shoulder. "Which book would you recommend for a romance novice?"

My preferred genre was historical fiction, but for her, I was willing to give anything a try. Plus, I could use a little romance in my life.

"Hmm." Pam trailed her finger over the colorful spines before stopping on one in particular. She slipped the book off of the shelf and handed it to me. "This is one of my favorites. It's about aliens on an ice planet."

I looked down at the cover. There was a frozen tundra with a beautiful brown-haired woman and a giant, blue alien male.

A little far-fetched, but okay.

I flipped it over and read the blurb. "Oh, this does sound good. I think I'll get it."

The look she gave me was priceless. Like I was some sort of saint for taking an interest in the things that interested her. Little did she know, I wanted to know everything I could about her. Everything we could possibly cram into this short period of time together.

For thirty minutes, we browsed the bookstore. I offered to hold Pam's selections for her, watching as she piled title after title into my arms until the stack almost reached my face.

"I think I might have gone a little overboard," she said, her brows raised as she peeked over the books at me.

"Nonsense. I think this is the perfect amount."

We walked over to the counter and I placed the books down for the cashier.

"Is this everything?" the cashier asked.

"Yep, that's everything. We made sure we left a few books in the store for you, though," I teased, and Pam nudged my arm playfully.

She went to put her card down, but I stopped her once again.

"Pam," I said as I looked down at her. "Please let me get these for you. Consider it a late Christmas present—if you celebrate Christmas, that is."

"Alistair..."

"Please. I want to. That way, when you read them, you'll think of me."

"Fine," she said with a smile that made my heart race.

Oh, this was bad.

I was in serious trouble.

With a heavy bag of books on my arm, I held the door open for Pam as we made our way back onto Main Street.

"Did you drive here?" I asked.

"I walked, actually. I live on one of the side streets."

"Are you still up for ice skating?" I was hoping she'd say yes.

Please fucking say yes.

"Absolutely. You aren't getting rid of me just yet."

I felt like I'd won the lottery.

"The rink is at the park. Would you be alright with me driving us over?"

Since we'd just met, I wasn't sure if she'd feel comfortable getting in the car with me. I'd heard those online dating stories on true crime podcasts. There were some real crazies out there.

"I trust you," she said, threading her arm through mine.

———

"WELL, it doesn't look like the ice skating rink is too popular today," I said as I pulled my car to a stop at the park.

Besides one car, which I assumed was the rink attendant's, the parking lot was empty.

"Hmm. It's a shame too. For January, it's actually a pretty nice day."

"Even though you almost slipped and fell on a patch of ice?"

She shrugged. "Gotta look on the bright side. The sun is shining, and I have great company."

I liked her attitude. Her positivity aligned well with my own.

I got out of the car and walked around to open the door for her.

"Thank you. You're such a gentleman."

"I had a good role model. My father treated my mother like a queen."

It was the truth. When I thought of the perfect couple and the ideal relationship, my parents always came to mind. It was the type of love I'd wanted with Chai's mother but could never find. After that, I sort of gave up looking, I guess.

"Alistair?" Pam looked up at me, her bright green eyes sparkling and her vibrant red hair blowing in the chilly wind. "Is everything okay?"

"Everything's fine. Better than fine, actually. Ready to do some ice skating?"

She nodded and I extended my arm out to her, but this time she wrapped her arm through mine *and* slipped her palm into my hand.

We were holding hands.

It was something so innocent—so normal—but with her, it felt *intimate*.

I puffed out my chest, my body buzzing with excitement as we walked hand in hand toward the skating rink.

"Hey, Mrs. Rollins." The skating rink attendant greeted us with a wave and a smile. It was like Pam was a local celebrity.

"Hi, Javier! Reece still has you working the rink, huh?" So the guy worked for her son... I expected her to drop my hand, but she didn't. Our fingers were still laced together tightly.

The handsome guy, Javier, shrugged. "I don't mind it too much. It's probably for the best. Reece isn't great with customer service."

The two of them laughed.

From the sound of things, her son was a bit of a grouch.

Based on her demeanor and what I'd heard about her daughter, I had a hard time believing it.

"Will it just be the two of you today?" Javier's eyes darted down to where our hands were joined.

I opened my mouth to answer, but Pam got her words out first.

"Yes, just the two of us." She smiled at me, the crow's feet in the corners of her eyes crinkling. It was the only place that hinted at her age, but I liked it. It showed that more often than not, you could find her smiling. "And before Alistair here gets his card out, I'd like to pay."

"No, no, no." Javier shook his head and held his hands up. "This one is on me." He gave me a sly wink. "What size skates for you, Mrs. Rollins?"

He passed us a dainty pair of size seven skates for Pam and a set of hoof adapter blades for me. They were like those old-timey roller skates that went over your shoes, but they were designed to fit hooved monsters. I was impressed the town had so many accommodations for its monster residents. They'd really welcomed monsters with open arms here in Briar Glenn.

"When was the last time you went ice skating?" Pam asked as she slid off her boots.

I puffed out a breath. "Let's see...Maybe ten years or so? Not since Chai was young, that's for sure."

Pam giggled. The redness on her cheeks and nose from the cold made it even more adorable. "Well, this should be interesting then. Do you want me to ask Javier for one of the skate trainers?"

"Pamela Rollins." I brought my hand up to my chest in mock offense. "Do you really think so little of my ice skating prowess?"

She snorted, the warm air shooting out of her nostrils. "Come on then, big guy. Show me your skills."

With perfect balance, she rose on the blades of her skates and extended a hand out to me. Holy goddess, next to her I was going to look like a bull in a china shop.

I stood on wobbly legs, my body used to balancing on flat hooves rather than a set of thin blades. Pam grabbed my hand before I could fall and embarrass myself.

"I've got you," she said with a genuine smile. "We'll go nice and slow so you can get used to it."

She stood in front of me, holding both of my hands as she skated backward. Meanwhile, I moved at a snail's pace, my giant body being dragged along by a tiny human woman.

The most beautiful human woman I'd ever seen.

"There you go," she praised. "Move your legs forward and back to push yourself along."

"O-okay," I stammered, following her instructions, slowly pumping my legs forward and back.

The tiny adjustment helped me go faster, which seemed to please Pam.

"That's it. Great job. I'm going to let go of one of your hands and skate alongside you now, alright?"

Completely focused on not falling, I gave her a nod.

Pam released one of my hands and carefully spun alongside me, matching the rhythm of her skates to mine.

"Look at you go," she encouraged as we made our way around the oval rink.

"I think I'm starting to get the hang of it now."

On our second lap, a crooning love song began to play from the speakers surrounding the skating rink.

Javier was really trying to set the mood. He was an A+ wingman.

"I love this song." Pam skated closer and wrapped her arm through mine.

At that moment, whatever newly learned balance and skating skills I had completely went out the window. My legs wobbled like a newborn fawn and as I fell down, I pulled Pam down on top of me.

"Shit," I groaned. "Are you alright?"

She pushed my curls out of my eyes and looked at me with concern written all over her face. "Am I alright? You're the one who fell on the ice. You cushioned my fall."

"You wouldn't have fallen if it weren't for me."

"Shh," she said and leaned in closer.

The sun shined behind her, setting her bright red hair ablaze in the afternoon light. I could feel the warmth of her breath on my nose. Tomorrow I'd be leaving, but I wanted this with her. Whatever this was between us, I was certain she felt it too.

It was now or never.

"Pam," I whispered. "Can I kiss you?"

Without saying a word, she brought her soft lips to mine, letting out a breathy sigh the moment we made contact. I was so in awe of her, aware of the press of her body over mine.

Her fingers tangled in the curls along the side of my face, her lips parting to allow me to deepen the kiss. The length of my snout made things difficult, but I was able to compensate with the finesse of my lips. I slid my tongue inside her mouth, slowly swirling the large, textured pad against hers.

"Hey! Are you guys okay?" Javier yelled across the ice from the attendant's booth.

Pam reluctantly pulled away, her dainty tongue darting out to lick her lips before she answered Javier.

"We're fine, honey. Alistair fell. I was just helping him up."

It felt like we were two teenagers who just got caught kissing. In a way, that's exactly what we were—two infatuated individuals caught in the moment.

I cleared my throat as Pam rolled off of me and helped me to my feet. While I fought to find my balance, my stomach let out an embarrassingly loud growl.

"Are you hungry?" she asked expectantly.

What were the odds that I could get her to have breakfast and lunch with me? We'd just shared a kiss, and I was in no rush to end our date.

"Yeah," I laughed awkwardly. "Just a little bit."

She grabbed my hand, rubbing her thumb over mine. "Would you want to come over to my place for lunch? I can make something or we can order take-out? I've been craving Chinese like you wouldn't believe."

Yes.

I was dying to see her place. To get to know her better.

"I'd love to."

Together, we skated back over to the bench and removed our skates to return them to Javier.

I placed the skates on the counter and Javier gave me a knowing smile.

"Did you two have fun?" he asked.

Pam's face flushed a deeper shade of pink, and we knew it wasn't because of the cold.

"It was great. Thank you so much, Javier."

Before he could say anything else, I grabbed Pam's hand and started the walk back to my car.

"Are you embarrassed he caught us?" I asked.

"You know, not really. I actually think it was sort of

thrilling." She nuzzled deeper inside of her scarf, refusing to look at me.

I stared at her with raised brows.

Was Pam Rollins a closet exhibitionist?

I wanted to find out, but we needed more time.

I'd make the most of this, though. That kiss would be lingering in my mind for a long time.

"Where to, pretty lady?" I asked as I climbed into the driver's seat.

"Do you know where Maple is?"

"Mmhm," I said with a nod.

"Sixteen-hundred Maple Street. You can pull into the driveway behind my car."

Her hand slid across the center console, settling over top of mine before giving it a little squeeze.

Like I said, trouble.

FIVE

PAM

"Living in the moment is being aware of the moment we are in. If our minds are in the past or future, we are not truly alive in the present." - Satsuki Shibuya

---

"I hope you like cats," I told Al as I pushed open the front door.

Just as I suspected, Remi was there and ready to greet us. As far as cats went, he was extremely friendly. He thought any visitors were there for him and him alone.

"Oh my goodness," Al cooed. "Who is this?" He knelt in the entryway, allowing Remi to rub against his hand.

It was a welcome surprise. Not everyone was a fan of cats, let alone Sphynx cats. The whole hairless thing was a big ick factor for a lot of folks.

"That's Remi." I looked down at the two of them and smiled.

"He's adorable. I love his little sweater. Did you make that?"

Oh no. Did I out myself as a crazy cat lady?

"Yeah," I mumbled under my breath. "I know, it's kind of sad." I could feel a blush creeping up my throat and over my cheeks.

Al stood and moved into my space. "I happen to think it's very cute." He grabbed my waist, my pulse pounding as he pulled me tight against him.

"I think you're very cute."

He leaned down and nuzzled my hair with his soft pink nose. "Do you, now?"

"Mhmm." Whatever cologne he wore smelled amazing, like a forest full of sage and cedar, what I imagined his home in the mountains of Colorado smelled like.

"Can I kiss you again?" he whispered.

Kissing someone with a snout was different, but when Alistair drew his lips together, he could mold them to mine perfectly.

"Please," I rasped on a heavy exhale.

The moment our mouths made contact, he groaned and tugged me closer. I parted my lips on a heavy breath, letting him slip his wide tongue inside my mouth. Our hands explored one another, sliding over our clothes with a sense of desperation that came with having a timeline. We were both acutely aware of the fact that this was temporary, but we wanted it, *wanted each other*, anyway.

As our kiss grew frantic, I could feel the swell of his cock against my stomach.

It was *big*.

Intimidatingly big.

I had only ever been with Don, and he certainly hadn't been as well endowed as Alistair.

Curiosity got the better of me.

My hand slid down Alistair's chest, over his belly, and

came to rest on top of his cock. I rubbed it through the thick material of his jeans, and he groaned into my mouth.

"Pam," he rasped, bucking his hips into my hand ever so slightly.

I pulled away and gazed up at him, my teeth digging into my lower lip. "Can I suck your cock?"

I firmly believed that if you wanted something, you should ask for it.

Al's expression softened, his big brown eyes full of concern. "Pam, you don't have to..."

"I-I want to. I hope that isn't too forward."

He cupped the side of my face with one of his massive hands. "Not at all. I just don't want you to feel pressured into doing something you don't want to do."

"I want this," I said, massaging the swell of his cock again. I could imagine it filling my mouth, the soft glide of his shaft over my lips...

"Fuck, okay," he breathed.

I grabbed his hand, leading him to the living room.

He sat on the couch and loosened his belt. "Are you sure?"

I knelt in front of him and nodded my head. I hadn't been so sure of something in a long, long time.

Alistair worked his jeans and underwear down, allowing his cock to spring free.

"Holy goddess," I whispered as I took in the sight before me.

Just as I'd expected, his body was covered in a layer of thick, curly hair.

But his cock?

I'd never seen anything like it.

The light pink shaft emerged from a fuzzy sheath located between his legs. It was long and smooth, with a slight upward curve that tapered to a pointed uncircumcised tip. A set of heavy, orange-sized testicles sat just underneath it, *also covered in hair*.

Concern flashed over his face when he noticed I was staring. "Is everything alright?"

Yep, just impressed by your massive minotaur dick. Nothing to see here.

"More than alright," I reassured him, and leaned in closer, bringing my mouth toward the already weeping tip.

"Hey." With his free hand, he tilted my chin up, urging me to look at him instead of his cock. "Take it nice and slow, okay? And if at any point you want to stop, we can stop."

"Okay."

He smiled, and I ran my fingers over his fuzzy thighs, making his body quiver before I drew him into my mouth.

I was wildly out of practice, but I continued working him toward the back of my throat. In addition to being long, his cock was *thick*, stretching my mouth around it made my lips tingle.

"Shit," he groaned. "That feels amazing."

Good.

I picked up the pace, bobbing up and down until spit ran down my chin and the fur of his sheath tickled my face.

"Yes, Pam. Just like that," he grunted, thrusting his cock deeper. "Can I touch you?"

"Mhmm," I hummed around his cock.

One of his hands fisted my hair, drawing me back. He was in charge of the pace now, forcing me to suck him nice and slow. I reached between his legs and cupped his balls, massaging them in the palm of my hand as best as I could.

"Fuck. Fuck," he panted with heavy breaths.

He liked that.

His grip on my hair tightened and he pushed me down

onto his cock before quickly pulling me back up. I felt his balls tense in my hand—he was getting close.

"Pam," he groaned. "I'm going to come. Do you want to taste me, babe?"

"Mhmm," I mumbled, sucking so hard my cheeks hurt.

"Damn." Alistair stared down at me in awe. "You look so pretty with your mouth around my cock."

I clenched my thighs, my pussy throbbing from his compliment.

He closed his eyes and fucked my mouth, his hips snapping in unison with the bobs of my head.

"Yess," he hissed.

His cock jerked as he came, the sweet, milky flavor of his cum filling my mouth to the point where I had difficulty swallowing, leaving some to drip down his shaft.

I worked his balls until he stopped moving, ensuring I got every last drop of cum out of him.

When I finally slipped him out of my mouth, he was still unbelievably hard.

"Was that okay?" I asked, wiping my lips with the hem of my sweater. I got him to come, and he seemed to enjoy it, but I wanted to hear it from him.

"Okay?" he asked and threw his head back against the headrest of the couch. "It was more than okay."

My eyes locked on his still-erect cock. "You're still hard though..."

One of his eyes peeked open and he smiled. "I'm a minotaur bull, babe. We can go up to twenty times a day."

Twenty times a day.

A deep laugh vibrated out of him as he tucked his cock into his pants. "It'll go back in soon. Do you want to lie down so I can reciprocate?"

I worried my lip, thinking it over. It was sweet of him to

offer, but I wasn't really used to receiving when it came to oral sex.

"No, that's okay. I, um, I'd love to cuddle, though." I was hoping he'd agree. I wanted to snuggle up against that big, warm minotaur body of his like a kitten.

"Come here," he said with a smile.

I stood, groaning as my knees cracked on the way up. I was about to cozy up next to Al on the couch when *he pulled me into his lap.*

"How's this?" he asked, his hands gripping my ass tight.

I stared at him with wide eyes. I wasn't used to being in someone's lap. Not at my age. *But I liked it.* "Good." I placed my head on his chest and snuggled closer. "Do you want to order food?"

"Oh, yeah. I got distracted."

I snorted. "Sorry about that."

His thumb traced lazy circles over my hip. "I like it when you do that."

"Do what?"

"The snort you do when you laugh sometimes. It's adorable."

I'd always thought it was dorky or unladylike. Don had certainly never commented on it one way or another, but here was Alistair on our first date, telling me he liked it. It was enough to make butterflies flutter in my stomach.

"Thank you," was all I could manage. Normally, I was better at receiving compliments, but there was something different about it coming from Al.

"You're welcome." He wrestled his phone out of his pocket, taking care not to jostle me too much. "Does the Chinese food place have online ordering?"

"Yep." I nodded my head against his chest. The fluffy

patch of hair sticking out from beneath his shirt tickled my nose, and I sucked in a deep inhale of his woodsy scent.

"What's it called?"

"King's." I stifled a yawn. The events of the morning, combined with the warmth radiating off Alistair, made me feel like I could have fallen asleep right then and there.

"No yawning, sleepy head. We have to eat first. What do you want?"

"Umm, shrimp fried rice and an eggroll. Oh, and crab rangoons."

He laughed, the puff of air from his wide nostrils ruffling my bangs. "Of course we need crab rangoons. Anything else?"

I thought for a second. Something sweet would balance out all that sodium. "Can you get me a Dr. Pop?"

"That sounds good. We'll make it two. What's your address again?" One of his hands drifted over my back, his finger trailing up and down my spine while he waited for me to reply. It was such a tender caress from someone so *large*. Alistair might be a giant minotaur bull, but he was so gentle.

"Sixteen-hundred Maple Street," I said sleepily, my fingers running through the soft hair covering his chest. It made sense that he was so warm, he had a permanent sweater on.

"Alright. Food is ordered." Al sat his phone on the couch cushion next to us and wrapped his arms around me. He leaned down, the velvety skin of his nose nuzzling against my temple. "This is nice."

"It really is," I said with a breathy sigh.

But it was bittersweet because it was only temporary. It would be over before it could even get started.

"Al, I—"

"Shh," he murmured, his soft lips caressing my face. "Let's just enjoy it. Just be in the moment with me, Pam."

Just be in the moment with me, Pam.

I couldn't remember the last time I was asked to be present. Or was the center of someone's moment.

I sank down into Al, doing as he asked. We sat there with me snuggled on his lap, not speaking, just feeling our hearts beat and listening to one another breathe.

SIX

ALISTAIR

"I am tomorrow, or some future day, what I establish today. I am today what I established yesterday or some previous day." - James Joyce

---

"Pam," I whispered when I heard a knock at the door. "Pam, I have to move you. The food is here." In the thirty minutes we'd been waiting for our take-out order, she'd fallen asleep on my chest, and I hadn't had the heart to wake her. She was so peaceful. It was adorable.

"Okay." She sighed, rolling off me and onto the couch.

I gave her leg a tiny caress before getting up to answer the door.

A lanky, college-aged kid greeted me when I opened it. "Delivery for Alistair."

"Yep, that's me."

He passed me the food. "Thanks for the tip. Have a great day, man."

"You too."

Pam was still on the couch where I'd left her, so I wandered around the house looking for her kitchen. Her place was so cozy. Family photos covered the hallway walls, and I stopped to get a better look at them.

There were tons of pictures of her kids: Reece standing tall with a trophy from a softball tournament, Tegan riding a pony, both kids enjoying ice cream cones as they dripped down their hands.

There were also some photos of *him* with the kids.

Her late husband, Don.

In most of the pictures, he had an ugly scowl on his face. He wasn't an unattractive guy—he was actually pretty handsome—but I got a sense from the photos that he had an ugly personality. It made me sad all over again that Pam had spent so many years of her life with him when the short period of time I had with her was slipping away.

All I knew was if I'd had a woman like that as my wife, I would have treated her how she deserved to be treated. I would have let her know every day how lucky I was to have her in my life. Pam Rollins was really something else.

Remi rubbed against my leg.

"Hey there, little buddy. Where's the kitchen in this place?" I knew some people thought talking to animals like they were people and asking them questions was silly. But I'd always found them to be understanding and responsive in their own way.

Remi proved my point, weaving through my legs and leading me down the hall to the left—straight to the kitchen.

"That's a smart boy," I said, scratching him under the chin.

Gods, maybe if I had a cat, my life wouldn't be so lonely.

I sat the food on the kitchen table, then searched through the cabinets and drawers. When I had our places set and the food laid out, I went to wake up Pam.

She looked beautiful as she slept there on the couch. The warm glow of the late afternoon sun slipped through the blinds, highlighting her hair a brilliant ruby red. I thought about taking a picture but decided against it. It was sort of creepy to do something like that, especially on the first date. Instead, I closed my eyes and took a deep breath, committing the way she looked to memory, vowing I'd never forget.

"Pam," I whispered. "Pam, the food is here." I ran my hand over her leg, giving it a gentle shake.

Her eyes fluttered open, vibrant emeralds peeking up at me from beneath heavy eyelids. "Shit. I'm sorry. I didn't mean to fall asleep. I was just really comfortable. You're so warm."

She had nothing to apologize for. I loved that she felt comfortable enough with me to fall asleep in my lap. It had been such a long time since I'd shared a moment like that with someone. "There's nothing to be sorry about, sweetheart." I extended my hand out to her. "Come on, let's eat. Remi is in the kitchen waiting for us."

Pam shook her head and took my hand. "That cat is such a mooch."

"He's cute, so he can get away with it."

She laughed as we walked down the hall to the kitchen. "Don't tell me he's already got you wrapped around his little hairless paw."

I shrugged, my wide frame rubbing against Pam's arm in the narrow hallway. "What can I say? I can't resist good pussy."

Pam snorted, her cheeks beet red, and her mouth hanging open. "Alistair!" She nudged my hip playfully, and I roared with laughter.

"I'm sorry. I couldn't help myself. It was just too good."

The moment we entered the kitchen, she stopped dead in her tracks and gripped my arm.

"You set the table for us?" I could have sworn her eyes twinkled as she stared up at me.

It was the bare minimum I could do, yet she acted like it was some grand gesture. Her late husband had really done a number on her. That guy had no idea how lucky he'd been to have her as a partner. If I were ten years younger... If I didn't live halfway across the country...

I ran my palm over Pam's cheek, giving her a small smile and willing all the sadness I felt away. "I did. Have a seat, hun." I pulled out the chair in front of her place setting, motioning for her to sit.

"Thanks," she said as she scooched in. "I take it you found everything okay?"

"I did." I nodded, sitting across from her. "You have a lovely home."

"Thank you. We had it remodeled once the kids moved out. I've thought about downsizing now that Don is gone, but I can't seem to part with the place. It was originally my great-aunt's. She left it to me when she passed."

"I love that." It wasn't something you saw a lot of these days. When a loved one passed and left something to their family, they'd just sell it off, favoring shiny new construction over an old family home. I liked that this house meant something to her.

"What did you get?" Pam asked as she scooped her shrimp fried rice onto her plate.

"General Tso's Tofu. It had a ton of five-star reviews."

"Huh. Never tried it."

"Would you like to?" I asked, spearing a piece of tofu on my fork.

She peered across the table at my plate for a moment. "Actually, yeah. I'd love to. Maybe it'll be my new favorite."

The table was small enough that I could hold my fork out and place it into her mouth. My eyes widened as I watched the food slip inside her mouth, her soft lips closing over the fork as I pulled it away.

I was reminded of how pretty she looked with her lips wrapped around my cock like that. How eager she was to taste me, *to please me*.

"Oh wow," she said through a mouthful of food. "This is really good. I've been missing out."

I took a bite, the spicy-sweet flavor coating my tongue. "Damn. That is good. Here." I grabbed the container and scooped some onto Pam's plate.

"Thank you for sharing with me."

I smiled at her. "You're always welcome to anything that's mine."

WE TALKED WHILE WE ATE, our late afternoon lunch continuing into the early evening. The food was so delicious that I'd overindulged.

"Ugh," I said, sliding my chair back from the table. "I ate too much."

Pam looked at my empty plate and chuckled. "The next time you're in town, you'll know where to order from."

Her comment seemed to ground us both. I was just a visitor here, not a permanent fixture in this town or her life. It hurt more than it should, at least this early on. I mean, shit, we were on our first date. Chai was wrong. It wasn't Pam who was catching feelings and having her heart broken. It was me.

Pam's phone chimed from the other room.

"Ope," she said as she rose from the table. "That's probably Tegan. I told her I would call and let her know how the date went. She's probably concerned that she hasn't heard from me. I'll be right back." Without another word, she bustled down the hall in search of her phone.

Her daughter likely didn't expect our date to be an all-day affair. Honestly, I hadn't either, but now that we were here, I didn't want it to end.

Remi rubbed against the leg of my pants before jumping onto my lap.

"Hey, buddy." I ran my hand over his sweater-covered back, eliciting a deep purr. "You take care of your momma when I'm gone, okay? She's a special lady."

He stuck his tail straight up and started to make biscuits on my lap. It wasn't a direct yes, but it was good enough for me.

Pam turned the corner and smiled when she caught sight of me loving on Remi. "I am so sorry about that. I didn't want her to worry."

"No reason to be sorry. Did you tell her how it was going?"

"Yep. I told her you were the most handsome minotaur I'd ever seen." She paused for a moment. "And I told her about the kiss. I thought it was better that she heard it from me instead of Javier."

That was right. Javier worked for her son. Reece was probably already aware of our little PDA session. I just hoped he didn't give Pam a hard time over it. She was a grown woman. She deserved affection.

"Oh?" I looked at her with my brows raised. "What did she have to say about that?"

"She was excited. She thought it might be a little fast, but I reminded her about Atlas mating her within a week of knowing her. It drove home the point pretty quick."

It made me wish minotaurs had fated mates like wolven. Unfortunately, it wasn't a thing for our kind.

"Is everything okay?" She stood next to my chair, her hands tousling my curls as she massaged the base of my ears.

"Mmm," I groaned. "That feels good."

"I was thinking we could watch a movie together. Maybe cuddle a little bit. Unless you have somewhere to be, that is."

I closed my eyes and leaned into her touch. "Pam Rollins, for today, I am all yours."

"Good. Let's get in my bed."

My eyes darted open, and Remi jumped from my lap. "Y-your bed?" I stammered in disbelief.

She wanted me to get in her bed with her?

"I am so sorry. I thought you'd be more comfortable there instead of the couch. I don't think there's room for us to cuddle." Her cheeks were bright red as she awkwardly backed away.

"Hey." I grabbed her hand and pulled her closer to me. "I didn't mean it like that. I was just surprised, that's all. I'd love to lay in bed with you."

The blush across her cheeks began to fade, and the corners of her soft lips tilted up into a smile. "Let me get this cleaned up first. I don't want Remi getting into anything."

It sounded like her little Sphynx cat was quite the rascal. I'd always considered myself a dog person, but he was making me rethink my ways.

"I'll help." I closed the Chinese food containers and gathered up the plates and silverware.

"Are you always this helpful?" she asked with a laugh, taking the dishes from me and giving them a quick rinse before placing them inside the dishwasher.

I shrugged. "Like I said, my parents were good role models for what a relationship should be. I also live alone, so I'm used to cleaning up after myself. If I don't do it, who will?"

Granted, I did have a housekeeper, but she took care of the deep cleaning. I was responsible for the day-to-day stuff, like the dishes and wiping down the counters.

"That's true. I'm just not used to it, that's all. Even though I worked, Don still expected a lot from me in terms of housework. He was pretty old-fashioned."

I shook my head in disgust.

Don.

From the sound of things, I'd treated her better in one day than he had their entire marriage. It was enough to make me see red, but it quickly passed when Pam grabbed my hand and led me toward the stairs. It had been so long since I'd been in bed with a woman. Even if this was something as innocent as relaxing and watching a movie.

Was it innocent, though?

Pam had initiated giving me head earlier. Maybe this was her hinting that she wanted more.

She was the one in charge here. I was down for whatever she was comfortable with.

"Here we are," she said, flipping on her bedroom light. It was only four but her room was already dim with shadows.

Pam's room was exactly as I'd expected. A neatly made king-size bed sat in the center of the room. The wall behind it was painted a muted sage green that worked well with the cream-colored knit bedding. A shelf sat above the bed, holding a philodendron, some photographs, and various romance titles. A flat-screen hung over a shabby chic dresser directly across from the bed. It was feminine and cozy—just like Pam.

She turned on the lamps on either side of the bed, bathing the room in a warm glow. "Much better," she said with a smile before climbing into bed.

I shifted my weight nervously and looked down at my hooves. They were coated in a layer of salt crystals from our walk. There was no way I was getting in Pam's bed like that. "Do you have a towel I can wipe off my hooves with? I don't want to get your bed all dirty."

Pam shot out of bed so fast. "Oh my gosh. I'm so sorry. Let me get you a towel." She ran into the adjoining bathroom, and I heard the faucet.

"It's fine. I wouldn't expect you to consider these sorts of things about minotaurs right away," I called out to her.

She walked out of the bathroom and over to me, damp towel in hand. "I know...But I want you to feel welcome here." She handed me the towel. "I want you to be comfortable."

"Pam, I promise you. I'm very comfortable around you." I sat down on the bed and, with some difficulty, brought one of my hooves up to my lap. I wasn't as flexible as I used to be. I made a mental note to add 'daily yoga' to my New Year's resolutions list.

She watched with interest as I wiped one hoof and then the other. It was the first time she'd seemed curious about the monstrous parts of me, the parts that were different from humans. Well, interest in a monstrous part aside from my cock.

"You never wear shoes?" she asked as I passed her the towel.

I made myself comfortable on the bed, propping up on one elbow to stare at her while she threw the towel in the hamper. "No, not really. Most minotaurs don't. They make them, but we generally prefer our hooves. It makes balancing easier. Plus, they make that cool clacking noise."

"It is a cool noise." She gave me a wide smile before joining me on the bed.

I held my arm out, allowing her to snuggle against my chest.

"This is nice," she said, wrapping one of her arms over my chest, hugging me tight.

"It is." I took a deep breath, inhaling her scent and reveling in the closeness. I couldn't remember the last time I'd cuddled with someone.

"Can you pass me the remote? It should be there on the nightstand."

Doing my best not to disrupt her, I carefully stretched and grabbed the remote.

"Thank you. What do you want to watch?" she asked as she turned on the TV.

Truly, I didn't care what we watched. We could turn it off and sit in silence for all I cared. As long as she was here with me, *like this*, I was content.

Pam scrolled through the movies until she hovered over the title of an old comedy. "I do like this one. Will Ferrell and John C. Reilly are so funny."

"I like this one too. I was tempted to make the pan, Pam dilemma joke this morning."

She vibrated with laughter and started the movie.

"See! You would have got it. Missed opportunity."

Pam turned her head so she was gazing up at me. "You're always so funny, you know that? I love it."

I couldn't help but grin. "I'm glad because I love making you laugh." I leaned over, placing a gentle kiss on her head as the movie started.

SEVEN

PAM

I feel beautiful, I am beautiful.

Other than the glow of the bedside lamps, the room was dark.

The movie was over.

Beneath me, Alistair's chest rose and fell with a steady rhythm.

We must have fallen asleep.

I shifted, trying to reach my phone to check the time, but Al held me tight and rolled over top of me.

"Pam," he sighed in my ear, and I could feel the press of his thick cock against my pussy.

"Alistair," I whispered against his lips, feeling the soft tickle of his whiskers.

"Is this okay?"

"Yes."

His fingers trailed up the column of my neck. "Can I kiss you?"

"Please."

Things between us were moving at warp speed, but I felt comfortable with Alistair. He was big on consent which was important to me.

Alistair's fingers fisted in my hair, gently pulling my head to one side as he kissed up my neck.

"Fuck," I moaned, arching my back into his body.

"Someone likes neck kisses." I could hear the smirk in his voice.

He kissed along my jawline before pressing his mouth to mine. I parted my lips and slipped my tongue inside his mouth, feeling the warm pressure of his textured tongue against mine.

Don had never been big on oral sex, but I was insanely curious about what Al's tongue would feel like sweeping back and forth over my clit.

My hands traveled down to the bulge in his pants, stroking his cock through the material before fiddling with his belt buckle.

He broke the kiss and glanced down at me. "Pam, we don't have to—"

"Al. Please. I want this. If you want to, that is."

I was so turned on. It was our first date, and I was ready to beg him to sleep with me.

"Are you sure?" His deep brown eyes looked into mine, seeking confirmation that this was what I wanted.

"I don't think I've ever been more sure of something."

He thrust his hips against mine and smiled mischievously. " You want to feel this thick cock inside of you?" he asked with another thrust, and my breath hitched. "You want me to give you my cum?"

I nodded my head.

"Let's get undressed," he rasped against my neck.

Alistair rose from the bed and undid his belt, letting his jeans drop to the floor. Embodying confidence, he held my gaze as he unbuttoned his flannel shirt, his tail leisurely swishing back and forth behind him. I stared wide-eyed at the sight in front of me. Those tree trunk thighs, his perfect dad bod covered in soft hair.

"Come on," he said when he was stripped down to his boxer briefs. "Let me see you."

I took a deep breath and climbed off the bed, doing my best not to focus on the bulge in his underwear. Yeah, I'd already seen his cock, but that didn't make it any less impressive.

Slowly, I worked my leggings down, feeling thankful I'd shaved my legs. Once I'd kicked them off, I pulled my sweater over my head, revealing what was underneath.

I stood there in my black support bra and full-coverage cotton underwear, my soft body streaked with stretch marks, age spots, and cellulite. But I didn't feel self-conscious, not with the way Alistair looked at me.

He gazed at me with complete and utter adoration as he palmed his cock. "You're so beautiful. You know that, Pam Rollins?"

"Thank you." I didn't even refute it. I took the compliment because I *felt it.*

Alistair stepped closer. His fingers explored my body, the skin beneath pebbling in their wake. Carefully, he undid my bra, exposing the hardened tips of my nipples. He hooked his fingers into the waistband of my underwear, pulling them down as he lowered to his knees in front of me.

"Holy goddess," he said, nuzzling the velvety tip of his nose against my soft stomach. "So sexy."

He dragged his lips lower until I could feel the warmth of his breath over my pussy.

"I want to taste you, if that's okay." He tilted his head back to look up at me, checking in with me like he'd done all day. "But I understand if you don't like—"

I cut him off before he could continue. "No. No. It isn't that. It's just that—I don't have a lot of experience with someone going down on me." Admitting it was slightly embarrassing, but if anyone would understand and withhold judgment, it was Alistair.

"Pam." He gripped the back of my thighs, holding me tight. "You deserve pleasure. You deserve to be treated like the goddess you are. Let me give you that."

"Okay," I said, rubbing the base of his ears as I nodded in confirmation.

"Lie down on the bed for me, sweetheart." He placed a soft kiss on the bare skin of my pussy, easing some of my anxiety before he pulled away.

With a deep breath, I climbed onto the bed and spread my legs wide, baring myself to Alistair. Teasing the peak of my nipple with one hand, I slid the other over my stomach and into the slick heat of my pussy while I waited for him to join me.

Alistair's soulful eyes tracked every slip, slide, and glide of my fingers. He was completely focused on me as he pulled down his boxer briefs, releasing his cock. "That's it. Let me see that pretty pussy. Show me exactly what you like," he said, his voice raspy and rough.

I circled my clit, applying rough pressure as he worked his cock with slow strokes. "Alistair," I whined and threw my head back.

He was so confident. So sexy. And his tongue—I wanted to feel it.

The bed dipped as he joined me and settled his broad body between my legs, spreading me wider to accommodate his horns. Eyes locked with mine, Alistair grabbed my hand, bringing my fingers to his mouth and licking them clean.

"Shit," I gasped, forcing a laugh out of him.

I'd never seen something so—*sexy*.

"Did you like that, sweetheart? I've wanted to taste your pussy all fucking day."

"It was hot." The way my chest heaved with each word was evidence of that.

"Do you want me to keep going?" he asked, the cool kiss of his nose ring tickling my inner thighs.

"Gods yes." The words had barely left my lips when I felt the first swipe of his tongue along my center.

It felt so fucking good. Warm and wet and coarse, like nothing I'd ever experienced before.

Even my toys paled in comparison.

Alistair swirled his tongue in slow circles around my clit, getting close but never touching it, edging me with languid licks until I bucked my hips in frustration. I was so used to pleasuring myself that I was having trouble letting go.

He let out an amused laugh and wrapped his hands around the back of my thighs, giving him better control. "Patience, babe. Relax and enjoy it."

With another teasing swipe of his tongue, he finally reached my clit, dragging the wide pad over it again and again. Somehow, Alistair knew just how I liked it, applying heavy pressure instead of a tickling caress.

"Alistair," I breathed, my core already tightening.

"Does that feel good, sweetheart?" he asked.

"Yes," I moaned and reached down, grabbing his horns while I rode his face.

"That's it. Take what you need," he groaned between each lap of his tongue.

He was eating my pussy like I was a Michelin Star meal.

Alistair latched onto my clit with his lips, sucking hard, and that was it.

"Fuck!" I screamed as I tipped over the edge, my thighs quaking against his face with my orgasm.

It was intense, sending wave after wave of pleasure coursing through my body. It was better than anything I'd been able to give myself, especially since menopause.

And definitely better than Don had ever made me feel.

He continued to gently lick my clit until my body softened, and I released his horns.

"What do you think?" he asked, smirking up at me. He was obviously pleased with himself. "Can you give me another one?"

His fingers pushed inside of me before I could answer, drawing a moan from me as he caressed my G-spot.

Could I go again?

Gasping, I gripped the sheets, focusing on how full I felt with his wide fingers inside me.

It was one night. One amazing date and one night together.

I could definitely go again.

"I-I can give you another one," I sputtered. "And—and then I want you to fuck me."

"Mmm," he said, rubbing his damp face along the soft expanse of my inner thigh. "I love a woman who knows what she wants and isn't afraid to ask for it."

He rubbed my clit again, making tiny figure eights with the tip of his tongue and mimicking the movement internally with his fingers. As sensitive as I was from the first orgasm, it was perfect. Each soft, gentle touch, each glide of his tongue, made my pussy throb.

There was no way I was already close again.

Given Alistair's sexual prowess, it was obvious that his experience far outweighed my own—but I didn't fucking care. At that moment, I had his full attention, and that's all that mattered.

He replaced his tongue with his thumb, pulling back to look at me while he soothed his finger over my clit. "I can feel you clenching my fingers, beautiful. I want to see how pretty you look when you scream my name. I want to watch you come undone against my fingertips."

I loved that he wanted to watch me, that his main focus was me and my pleasure. It was all the things I'd read about in my romance books—he was like a pleasure dom—deriving satisfaction from how good he made me feel.

He pressed down on my clit, quickly dragging his thumb back and forth, his wide fingers pumping in and out.

"Fuck," I moaned. Feeling my center tense, I arched my back and closed my eyes, waiting for my orgasm to sweep over me.

"Look at me, Pam," Alistair called from between my legs. "I want those pretty green eyes watching me while I make you come."

I forced my eyes open and peered down at him while he stroked my clit. The tips of his fingers curled over my G-spot again, and again, and again, until I cried out from the intensity of my orgasm.

"That's it," he purred. His movements slowed, and he withdrew his fingers. "You look so beautiful when you come for me."

Alistair peppered my inner thighs with soft kisses, then peered up at me with a smug smile on his face. "You alright up there?"

I let out a deep breath. "I think I had an out-of-body experience."

"That's exactly what I was working toward." He laughed and kissed up my body until he was resting on his elbows over me. I could feel the press of his hard cock against my stomach. "Do you have condoms?" he asked.

It was a valid question, but I'd only ever had one sexual partner in my long-term, monogamous marriage. When I'd finished menopause, I'd asked my doctor to screen me for STIs—just in case I decided to enter the dating pool again.

As it turned out, that was a smart move.

"I was screened when I finished menopause and was negative."

"I tested negative six months ago and haven't had any partners since then."

I bit my lip and peered up at him. "If you're okay without using one, so am I."

He groaned and rocked against me slightly, his cock jutting into me.

Fuck, I wanted him inside me.

"I am more than okay with that," he whispered against the shell of my ear. "I can't wait to see my cum dripping out of your pretty, pink cunt."

Yep. It was official. Dirty talk was my new kink. All those years of vanilla marriage, and this is what I'd been missing out on? It was a damn shame.

Alistair rubbed his cock along my sensitive pussy, notching it at my entrance but not pushing it inside.

"I'll go nice and slow. Let me know if it's hurting you and we'll stop, okay?" His brown eyes were full of kindness as he tenderly brushed my hair out of my face with his thumb.

I nodded, and slowly, he eased the tapered tip of his

cock inside of me. My breath hitched, and I grabbed fistfuls of his hair as my pussy stretched around him.

"Shit," he huffed and stared down at where we were joined. "You're so fucking tight."

"You're so fucking big," I groaned.

"Am I hurting you?" he asked, concern flashing over his face.

"No. No, it feels good."

And it did.

His cock was slick and smooth, gliding in with zero resistance, which shocked me. Since I'd hit menopause, I'd had some issues with dryness, but that wasn't the case tonight. It was like Niagara Falls down there.

Alistair pushed in further until he was buried deep inside me, and his sheath rubbed against the entrance of my pussy.

"Pam," he breathed, leaning in closer until the hair on his chest teased the hardened peaks of my nipples. His lips lingered over mine for a moment, then he started to thrust, swallowing the gasp that left me with the first pump of his hips.

I arched into him again, meeting his thrusts, my fists tightening their grip on his hair. He was stretching me, breaking me apart just to build me up again. Propping himself up on one arm, Alistair slid his hand down my chest to my breast. He pinched my nipple between his fingers, and I whined, throwing my head back.

"Do you like that, beautiful? You like me playing with your nipples while I give you my cock?" he asked, his gruff voice sending shivers down my spine.

A strained "Yes," was all I could manage. I'd never had sex like this. Never been fucked within an inch of my life.

He gave my nipple one last pinch before moving his

hand lower, down to the swell of my hips. His fingers dug into my skin, and he fucked me harder, driving my body into the bed.

With each snap of his hips, his sheath teased my clit, coaxing me closer to my orgasm.

There was no way this was possible.

There was no way Alistair could make me come three times in one evening—but he seemed determined.

Still inside me, he shifted back onto his knees and gently raised my hips. Thanks to the new angle and slight upward curve of his cock, I could feel each pass over my G-spot.

"Do you need a pillow?" he asked, still thrusting into me.

I shook my head. I was so close to getting off; it felt too good to even bother.

"So." A harsh thrust.

"Fucking." Another thrust.

"Sexy." The sound of his body pounding into mine was muffled by his hair. "You're going to give me another orgasm, and then I'm going to fill this tight cunt with my cum."

Alistair released one side of my hips and trailed his fingers down to my pussy. He rubbed what felt like two fingers along my entrance before swirling them over my clit.

"Oh gods," I panted, sensitive from the two orgasms he'd given me already.

He continued to thrust, his cock hitting my G-spot just right and those magical fingers massaging my clit exactly how I liked it.

Tension built low in my stomach, and I could feel my pussy tightening around his cock.

"One more, Pam. One more, and I'll give this greedy pussy my cum."

Fuck.

Alistair pinched my clit between his fingers, giving it a gentle tug that made me come. This orgasm was different —*softer*—with soothing waves of pleasure that started in my center and radiated through my entire body.

"Yes, fuck. You feel so fucking good," he grunted, fucking me through my orgasm.

My pussy clenched his cock, and it spasmed inside me, filling me with his cum just like he promised.

When he was finished, he leaned into me, his hot, panting breaths caressing the crook of my neck.

"Pam. Kiss me," he said, the words raspy as he fought to catch his breath.

I turned my head and pressed my lips to his, savoring the warmth of his body, the sweep of his tongue against mine, and the connection I felt with him still inside me. It was a lazy kiss, soft and sumptuous, just the two of us cherishing this moment together.

I didn't want it to end.

Eventually, Alistair pulled away, gently nuzzling me with his nose before propping himself on his elbows.

"Shit," he said, looking down between us. "I should have asked you to put a towel down."

I laughed and ran my fingers through the soft hair along his sides. "It's fine. I have a mattress protector."

"It's, uh..." His bovine ears folded over bashfully. "It's just a little messy. Let me get you cleaned up."

Alistair pulled out slowly and settled himself between my legs again.

Was he going to do what I thought he was going to do?

That would be a first. Don would have never...

He watched intently as his cum dribbled out of my pussy, down onto my ass and the bed.

"Such a pretty sight," he groaned, rubbing his face along my thigh.

I could have sworn he was going to lick his cum off of me, but instead, he took two of his fingers and pushed it back inside.

"Fuck," I hissed at the intrusion, drawing a laugh out of him.

He pulled his fingers out and leaned over me on one arm. "Open your mouth."

It wasn't a question or a suggestion, but a command.

I opened my mouth, and Alistair slid his fingers inside. My eyes snapped shut, and I moaned when the flavor of the two of us hit my tongue. This was one of the most erotic sexual experiences I'd ever had—and it was a one-time thing.

Alistair slowly withdrew his fingers, and when I opened my eyes, he smiled down at me. "You liked that, huh?" he asked with a dreamy lopsided grin.

"Let's just say this has awakened a lot of things in me."

He laughed before pressing a gentle kiss to my forehead. "I'm glad I could make you feel good. Now where can I find your towels?"

Such a gentleman.

"They're in the bathroom, on the shelf to the left."

With a heavy grunt, he climbed off the bed and strutted, *nude*, into the bathroom.

He was so hot.

His personality, his body, his skills in the bedroom—all of it was perfect. And tomorrow, he was leaving.

Alistair carried two towels over to the bed, and I forced myself to give him a little smile.

We'd just had mind-blowing sex. I didn't want to dwell on the fact that he was leaving tomorrow. I wanted to enjoy the time we had left.

"Spread those legs, sweetheart," he requested and gingerly wiped me clean. "Now lift your hips for me."

I propped myself up on my elbows and thrust my pelvis forward, earning a little smile from him. He carefully spread a clean towel out underneath me to cover any mess we'd left on the bed.

When he was done, he threw the dirty towel in the hamper and climbed back into bed with me.

"Is this okay?" he asked, snuggling behind me so that I was the little spoon.

"This is more than okay," I answered.

It was the most content I'd felt in a long time.

I inhaled deep whiffs of his sage and pine scent, hoping my sheets would smell like him tonight because tomorrow they'd be going in the wash.

Wiggling closer, I could feel the press of his stiff sheath against my backside.

Twenty times a day.

It was a shame we didn't have more time.

EIGHT

ALISTAIR

I make the best and most out of everything that comes my way.

"It's getting late," I said, trailing two fingers along the curve of Pam's breast.

"I know." She turned towards me, running her hands through my chest hair and snuggling closer. "I just don't want you to go."

"I wish I didn't have to, but I don't want Chai to worry."

Pam nodded.

"I'm going to miss you," I admitted, kissing the top of her head. My fucking chest ached at the very thought of leaving her, at the idea that this was the end of us.

"I'm going to miss you too. So much."

"Pam, uh, what do you want to tell our kids? They're going to ask about what happened."

We were both close with our children, but I wasn't sure how much of *this* we wanted to share with them.

Pam's hand stilled over my heart. "I mean, mine know about the kiss." She took a deep breath. "But I think I'd like to keep the fact that we slept together between us."

I couldn't blame her. I was the first partner she'd had since Don, and we'd slept together on our first date. I had no issue with that.

I was happy about it.

Some things are that much better when they're kept secret.

"I agree. I think it's for the best." I placed one more kiss on her head before rolling out of bed.

Pam followed suit, and I admired her nude form before she grabbed a robe from the back of the door and wrapped it around her.

We were silent while I got dressed, a sadness settling over us, making it difficult to speak.

As I finished buttoning my shirt, Pam stepped close and grabbed my hand.

"Ready?" she asked, her voice a low whisper.

I nodded, and we walked down the hall together, then descended the stairs.

"Come here," I said, pulling her to me while we stood in the foyer.

She wrapped her arms around my waist and placed her head on my chest. "Promise me you'll come back and visit."

I slid my hand underneath her chin, tilting her face up so she was looking at me. "I promise."

I leaned over and kissed her, using my actions to say everything I couldn't put into words.

This wasn't the end for us.

It couldn't be.

I wouldn't let it.

This was just the beginning.

Pam pulled away and looked at me, tears welling up in her eyes. "Can I text you?"

I had to fight back my own tears. I hated seeing her like this, knowing that I was responsible for causing her, *for causing us*, this pain. "Please text me. Call me. Send smoke signals. Whatever you want."

A tear trailed down her cheek, but she gave me a little laugh. "Thank you for today, Al."

"No, thank you, Pam. Truly. You're a wonderful woman, and I had an amazing day."

While I put on my coat, Pam dug through the bag of books.

"Here. I expect a play-by-play when you get around to reading it." She handed me the book about ice planet aliens, and I ran my hand over the cover.

Something to remember her by. I'd start it on the plane ride back to Colorado and text her as soon as I landed. "Thank you."

Pam glanced at where her scarf hung by the door. "I want you to have one more thing." She grabbed it and wrapped it around my neck.

"Pam, I can't take this," I said, rubbing the well-loved material between my fingers.

"Please. I want you to have it."

I put my hand on her waist and leaned over, bringing my face closer to hers. "Kiss me one more time," I whispered, brushing her hair away from her face. "Please."

She gripped the collar of my jacket, pulling me to her until our lips touched in a quick kiss. "Bye, Alistair," she whispered against my mouth.

"Bye, Pam."

I opened the door, giving her a wistful smile, before I stepped outside and closed the door behind me.

My eyes teared up as I started my car and pulled out of the driveway. Normally, I wasn't much of a crier, but this killed me.

This might have been goodbye, but this wasn't the end.

CHAI GREETED me the second I walked through the front door. "Hey there, Mr. Romance. That was quite the date you were on."

I hoped she didn't grill me too much. I wasn't in the mood. I really just wanted to go to bed.

I shrugged and took off Pam's scarf and my coat, tucking the book under my arm. "It was fine."

Chai gave me a sideways glance. "Just fine? You were out with Mrs. Rollins all freaking day, Dad. And I heard from Tegan that you kissed at the skating rink."

My tail twitched in annoyance. Pam and I were right to keep the fact that we'd slept together between the two of us.

"We did. We were caught up in the moment. That's all that happened." I stalked off to the kitchen, hoping it was the end of Chai's questioning, but she followed behind me.

"Dad..."

"What?" I huffed as I set the book on the table and poured myself a glass of whiskey. I needed a drink.

"Are you okay?" She seemed genuinely concerned.

I sat at the kitchen table and dug my palms into my eyes. "I really like her, Chai," I whispered.

"Oh, Dad," she said with a sigh and rubbed my back. "And I thought you'd be the one breaking hearts."

I snorted and took a deep swig of my drink. "Nope. Very much heartbroken."

Chai was quiet for a few minutes like she didn't know

what to say. I couldn't blame her. Here she was counseling her father, who was heartbroken after one date.

An amazing date with an amazing woman.

She sat down next to me. "You know, you don't have to leave."

I swirled my glass and peered over at her. "My business is in Colorado, honey. I have to go back."

"Maybe you do right now, but you've been working remotely for the past month, and it's worked out. Plus, you're going to have to retire at some point." She put her head on my shoulder. "I'm just saying that if you think this is something you want to pursue, you should go for it. Life is too short to live with regret."

I laughed and took another drink. "There you go with that advice again, kid."

"I'm good at giving it, bad at taking it." She stood up from the table and gripped my shoulder. "Just think about it, Dad. I love you."

I placed my hand over hers and gave it a little squeeze. "I love you too, honey."

NINE

PAM

Nothing can disrupt my peace.

"Mom!"

Tegan's all-too-familiar call pulled me out of sleep. I thought that when your kids moved out, these types of interruptions ended, but with mine, that didn't seem to be the case.

Realization hit me, and I bolted upright.

Tegan was here. In my house. And I was still in bed post-one-night-stand with her friend's father.

Fuck.

I couldn't remember if I'd cleaned up the house last night.

What if it smelled like sex in here?

Was that even a thing?

It had been so long that I wasn't really sure. Al did have a pretty distinct scent to him.

And the sheets!

One thing was for sure, I didn't want her in my bedroom.

"Just a second, honey," I yelled and jumped out of bed. Well, jumped out of bed as fast as I could with the unfamiliar discomfort I had going on between my legs.

"Watch out, buddy. Mom's gotta make the bed," I told Remi and shooed him away. He looked at me like I'd personally offended him before sprinting out of the bedroom to greet Tegan.

In a total state of panic, I threw the comforter over the mattress, giving it a hasty inspection to ensure there weren't any visible *fluids* on it.

I heard Tegan's footsteps on the stairs, and right as I slipped on my robe and closed the bedroom door, she met me in the hallway.

"Good morning, kissing lady," she said, flashing me a bright smile. "I need to hear all the juicy details!" She held up a paper bag and a drink carrier with two cups of coffee. "I brought breakfast!"

"Since when are you such a morning person?" I asked and slipped on my glasses. "You could have called first."

"I did." Tegan turned and walked down the stairs as I followed along behind her. "Three times, actually. I was a little concerned when you didn't answer."

I pulled my phone out of my pocket, and sure enough, three missed calls from Tegan but zero messages from Alistair. It was early in the day, but I still felt a pang of disappointment.

Following Tegan into the kitchen, I was pleasantly surprised to find it nice and tidy.

That was right.

Like the true gentleman he was, Alistair had helped me straighten up after our late lunch.

Tegan sat at the kitchen table, and I joined her, lowering myself into the chair with a wince.

Her green eyes narrowed. "Is everything alright, Mom?"

"Everything is fine," I said with a wave of my hand. "I must have hurt myself yesterday when we fell on the ice."

"Mother." Tegan passed me a cup of liquid gold and a breakfast sandwich. "I'm tired of playing telephone here. I need the details. This was your first date since Dad. This is a big deal."

My body stiffened at the mention of Don. In one day, Alistair had made me feel things I'd never felt the entire time I'd been married, and now I had to sit here with our daughter and recount my date with another man. It was weird, but she'd been the one encouraging me to do this...

"Well. It was amazing." I sipped my coffee as she stared expectantly, waiting for me to elaborate. "We talked for a long time in the coffee shop. He told me about the camping trips he takes in his RV and about his job. We went to the bookstore, and he bought me a few things. I convinced him to get that book—you know, the series I love with the blue aliens?"

Tegan leaned forward in her chair, her eyes wide. "He's seriously going to read about the cooties? I can't even get Atlas to do that, Mom."

Considering how obsessed with her Atlas was, it really said a lot.

"I think he will, too. He seems like a man of his word." I smiled, recalling Alistair's genuine interest in the book. "After that, he drove us to the ice skating rink. I was a little nervous when I saw that Javier was working, but he was really sweet to the two of us. He even played some music to set the mood. Al isn't a very good skater, so I tried to help him as best as I could. He slipped and pulled me down with him, and it just sort of—happened."

Tegan smiled at me dreamily with her face resting on her fists. "That is so freaking cute, Mom. It sounds like something from a holiday movie."

"I'd like to think it was less cheesy than a holiday movie," I said with a laugh. "Javier ruined the moment by checking to see if we were okay. Did he tell your brother?"

She grimaced and nodded her head. "Yeahhh. He did."

"And what did Reece have to say about it?" His relationship with Don had always been complicated. I wasn't sure how my son would feel about me entering the dating pool again—let alone kissing someone.

"He was actually really cool about everything. We just want you to be happy, Mom."

"Thank you, sweetie. It's nice to have that confirmation."

"So what happened after that?" she asked with her brows raised.

"After that, we came back here, ordered Chinese food, and watched a movie."

"Did you guys make out on the couch?"

I could feel my cheeks growing red, so I looked away. It wasn't exactly what happened, but she didn't need to know the details.

"Oh my gosh!" she cackled. "You're like me in my teenage years. So I take it he's a good kisser?"

"An excellent kisser," I mumbled against the lid of my coffee cup.

Tegan's expression dropped slightly. "Doesn't he go back to Colorado today?"

I gave her a slow nod, settling into the fact that this was over for now.

"And how do you feel about that, Mom?"

"I'd be lying if I said that I wasn't a little sad. I really like him," I sighed. "He told me he would text me."

"Has he?"

"Not yet."

"See, this is what I was worried about," she huffed. "I don't want you to get your heart broken."

"Honey, it was just one date and a few kisses. I knew going into this that it wasn't going to be forever. Maybe next time he visits, we'll go out again." My voice was hopeful, but I was trying to convince myself of that, not Tegan.

"Well," she said, rising from the table. "I think you should stay on the dating app. Keep your options open. And someone was telling me about a speed dating group in Rock Harbor."

"No. No way," I said firmly. "This little foray into dating is plenty."

What I really meant was I liked Alistair and I wasn't in a rush to meet anyone else.

"Righttt," she hummed with a knowing smile and gathered up her trash. "I gotta get going, but let me know if he texts you, okay?"

"Will do, baby. Thank you for breakfast."

She walked around to my side of the table and kissed my cheek. "And make sure you ice your hip or whatever. See the doctor if it keeps bothering you."

I almost laughed, but I held it in. If she only knew the source of my discomfort was from getting plowed by a well-endowed minotaur...

"Hey, now. If I remember correctly, I'm the parent in this relationship," I said, following her to the foyer.

"I'm allowed to worry, Mom. See you later!" Tegan put

her coat on, gave me a little wave, and slipped out the front door.

Well, that wasn't so bad, I thought to myself as I climbed the stairs. I didn't have much on the agenda for today—but after last night, stripping the bed was an absolute must.

Tegan hadn't pressed me as much as I thought she would, but I was sure I'd be hit with a barrage of questions the next time I saw Reece.

I checked my phone again, hoping for a message from Alistair, but still nothing. He was probably busy packing. Maybe he was spending time with his daughter before he left? Or maybe it was a casual 'I'll text you when I'm free' type of situation, and I'd read things wrong?

I was so out of my element with all of this.

Was there a 'The Complete Idiot's Guide To Dating After the Death of Your Spouse' book?

I'd have to check during my next volunteer shift at the library.

As I finished tugging the fitted sheet off the mattress, my phone vibrated with a text message.

Alistair: Are you home?

TEN

"The chance to love and be loved exists no matter where you are." -Oprah Winfrey

---

"What am I doing?" I asked myself as I looked at the bouquet of grocery store flowers sitting in the passenger seat of my rental car. I was cutting it dangerously close with my flight, but I didn't really give a shit.

Since last night, all I could think about was her. Her laugh, her smile, her scent—the way her body felt pressed against mine. I'd spent the entire morning waffling over whether it was appropriate to text her, and even then, I wasn't sure what I was supposed to say.

Something about this just felt so necessary. I wanted—no, needed—to show her how interested I was.

My nerves peaked as I turned onto her street, my clammy hands slipping along the leather of the steering wheel.

If this didn't go over well, that was the end of it. I'd board my flight with a bruised ego and call it a day.

I pulled into her driveway, and before I could even put the car in park, Pam walked out the front door and onto the porch.

Alright, Al. It's now or never.

Taking a deep breath, I grabbed the flowers and exited the car.

"Al, is everything alright?" she asked, her eyes darting between my face and the flowers.

"Pam, listen. I know my profile on Mate Match said I'm looking for something casual, but I like you. I mean *really* like you." I joined her on the porch and grabbed her hand. "I know you have your own life here, but I want to see where this goes. Date me, Pam Rollins. I'll understand if you say no because of the distance, but please just give me a chance?"

I held the flowers out toward her, and she looked at them, her mouth hanging open.

Was it shock? Surprise? Disgust? I couldn't really tell.

Right when I was about to pull back the bouquet and regret the entire thing, she took it from me and held it against her chest.

"Alright," she said with a nod and a watery-eyed smile.

"Alright?" I asked, sounding a little too eager.

"Mhmm. I'd love to date you, Alistair Reid. But I have to tell you, I've never done this before."

I laughed and leaned in closer. "That's alright because I've never done this before either. We'll figure it out together."

She stared down at the flowers. "I thought you were just going to stop messaging me and disappear."

"Gods, Pam. I'd never ghost you. Do you know how

many times I typed out a 'good morning' text earlier, then went back and deleted it? I didn't want to come on too strong. But you know—" My nose wrinkled, and I gestured to the flowers. "It, uh, seems like I'm doing that anyway."

She tilted her head and stared at me, her green eyes sparkling behind the lenses of her glasses. "I happen to think it's romantic."

"Well, let me up the ante."

Bending down, I threaded my fingers through her hair and kissed her—and I mean really kissed her. If I didn't have a flight to catch, I'd take her inside and...

"Shit," I mumbled against her lips. "My flight."

She pulled away and traced her fingers down my chest. "You should go. I don't want you to miss it."

I could see the pain in her eyes, but the longer we drew this out, the harder it would be.

"Alright," I said and nuzzled the side of her face. "But I promise I'll text you as soon as I can, okay?"

"Okay." She ran her hand through the curls along the side of my face and kissed my nose. "Have a safe flight."

"I will." Giving her one last smile, I darted off the porch and hopped in my car.

It was cute that she was worried about me.

I drove to the airport, returned my rental car, and barely managed to make my flight. I received some disgruntled stares from the flight attendants as they scanned my ticket and closed the door behind me.

"Excuse me," I mumbled as I shimmied my way down the aisle.

I hated flying.

Not because I feared the plane would crash or anything, but because it was so damn uncomfortable. The little tin cans in the sky weren't engineered for monsters and humans with larger bodies in mind. The airlines packed you in like sardines to make the largest profit they could. Sure, flying first class helped tremendously, but that wasn't cost-effective for most folks.

I pulled the blue alien book from my carry-on before shoving it into the overhead storage. When I told Pam I would read it on my return flight, I meant it. She enjoyed this book, and I wanted to know why; I wanted to be able to discuss it with her.

It wasn't long before we were in the air, and once the flight attendant brought me my drink order—a whiskey on the rocks—I dug into the book.

Gods, what an opening scene.

The alien woke her up by eating her out—and called her clit *a third nipple.*

A third nipple between her legs.

It was one of the most unhinged yet hilarious things I had ever heard. I couldn't believe that Pam, sweet stranger to oral sex Pam, read this sort of thing. It was funny, it was romantic, and judging by how tight my pants felt, *it was pretty fucking hot.*

I grabbed my phone, snapped a pic of my place in the book, and sent it to Pam courtesy of the in-flight Wi-Fi plan I'd purchased. She responded almost immediately.

> Pam: Oh my gosh. You're actually reading it. That's one of my favorite parts. 😄

> Me: I told you I was going to! It's a lot spicier than I anticipated.

She responded with the blushing smiley face emoji, which I could picture as her exact expression. Not wanting her to feel embarrassed, I quickly added—

Me: I'm enjoying it.

Pam: I'm glad. You have to finish it and read book two. That one is my favorite. Did you make your flight?

I pulled up my shopping app and searched for the second book in the series. I was enjoying this, and if book two was her favorite...

Purchased.

Me: Just barely. I'll be landing soon.

Pam: When you get home, will you send me pictures of your house? I want to see it.

My house.

I lived in a modern cabin perched on the side of a mountain. It had it all: sleek angles, cedar siding, a sundeck, huge windows, and a view that was to die for. Yet with each passing year, it felt less and less like home. That was typical, I guessed because I had no one to share it with. When I arrived home tonight—there would be no one there to greet me. No familiar face or affectionate touches, just silence.

But if I video chatted with Pam, it wouldn't be silent.

Me: We can video chat and I'll give you the grand tour.

Pam: I'd love that.

ELEVEN

PAM

If I can change my thoughts, I can change anything.

"Pamela Rollins. He showed up at your house with flowers, asked you to date him, and almost missed his flight? That sounds like something out of a romance novel!" Nancy said in a whisper that bordered on too loud.

After a week of dodging my responsibilities and spending most of my free time texting or video chatting with Alistair, I was finally back at the library for a volunteer shift. For the past hour, I'd been filling in my friend and coworker, Nancy, with all the details of what exactly had transpired since the New Year—and unlike with Tegan, I'd provided Nancy with all the juicy bits.

"I know," I sighed, recalling how romantic it was. "But I just don't understand why he'd do all this for me."

"*Why?*" Nancy gaped and leaned in closer. "You're an amazing woman with plenty to offer! You need to stop with all that negative self-talk. Hold on a second."

She slipped on her glasses from where they hung on a beaded lanyard around her neck and began typing furiously, searching for something in the library's database system.

"Aha!" she said after scrolling down the page and scribbling a number on a sticky note. "I'll be right back."

I watched her bustle off into the stacks, her bohemian skirt fluttering behind her. I loved how it was the dead of winter, and she was dressed like it was the summer of '69.

Nancy and I had been friends since middle school, but her life had gone in a drastically different direction than mine. She'd gone away to college, explored exotic places, and never married or had children. She was the free spirit to my homebody, and I appreciated her for it.

After a few minutes, she returned and handed me a book.

Finding Yourself After Forty: How Mantras, Meditation, and Daily Yoga Transformed My Life.

A self-help book?

She couldn't possibly be serious.

"Don't you do it. Don't look at me like that, Pam," she said, pushing the book toward me again. "I saw the author speak a few months ago in Santa Fe, and it was life-changing. Just take it home and read it. I really think it'll speak to you. Especially in your current situation."

I grabbed the book, flipping it over to find a woman our age dressed from head to toe in spandex, smiling at the camera as she held some elaborate yoga pose. "Nance, you know I'm not flexible. How is this supposed to help me?"

She laughed and shook her head. "I mean, yoga *would* help with your flexibility, but it isn't only about yoga. It's the mantras—the affirmations. Reminding yourself that you're worthy of good things."

"Reminding myself I'm worthy of good things, hmm?" As a mom, I constantly did that for my children, but when was the last time I'd talked myself up? When was the last time I truly believed I was something special?

Maybe my marriage had done more damage than I'd realized.

Nancy reached out and grabbed my hands where they rested on the book's cover, giving them a soft squeeze. "If anyone deserves a little romance, it's you. And maybe you'll be inspired to take up yoga. Work on your flexibility a little bit for Alistair."

"Nancy!" I choked out and swatted her arm, sending her into a fit of laughter that had the library patrons glaring in our direction.

"You never know. You're in for quite the workout if he can go twenty times—"

"Will you stop it!" I hissed. I could feel my cheeks growing hot with embarrassment.

She wiggled her eyebrows and slipped off her glasses, letting them dangle around her neck. "I'm just giving you a hard time. I'm happy for you, Pam. I really am. Alistair sounds lovely."

"He is. But the distance..." I thought about it more often than I liked to admit. It wasn't like I could just hop in the car and stop by his place whenever I wanted.

Nancy waved me off. "Distance is relative. You can be in the same room as your partner and feel like you're worlds apart. It's the connection that matters."

Well, she had me there. She'd summed up my entire relationship with Don in a few sentences. Alistair and I had a connection, that was for sure, but it was still in the early stages, where everything was shiny and new. How would we feel in a few weeks when the initial excitement faded, and the distance got to be too much?

Shit.

Here I was, self-sabotaging again, completely disregarding the fact that I was happy and worthy of good things.

"Alright. I'll read the book and let you know what I think." I checked out the book and slipped it into my bag, earning me a smile from Nancy.

"Thank you, and make sure you tell Mr. Darcy I said hello," she said with a wink and shrugged on her patchwork coat. "Did you want to grab a coffee?"

Our shift was over, and as much as I loved Nancy's company, I wanted to get home and laze around before my phone call with Alistair this evening.

"I can't today, but maybe later this week."

She sighed and wrapped the rainbow scarf I'd made her around her throat. "I see how it is. Already ditching your friend for your boyfriend."

"It isn't like that at all!" I laughed, even though it was *definitely* like that.

"Mhmm. Next thing I know, you'll be moving to Colorado and shacking up in a chateau with a millionaire minotaur, like in one of your books." Nancy threw her bag over her shoulder and gave me a quick hug. "I'll see you later this week!"

"See ya!"

While being whisked away to a mountain mansion would make for an amazing romance novel, it wasn't something I'd ever consider. My entire life was here. Tegan was getting married in the fall, and I was under the impression it wouldn't be long before she and Atlas made me a grandma. As for Reece and Cyrus, I knew they were just biding their time, letting Atlas and Tegan have their moment before they got engaged.

There was too much happening here for me to leave. Not even a charming minotaur could change that.

As I walked out to my car, my phone vibrated with a call.

Speak of the devil.

"Hey there, pretty lady," Alistair said on the other end of the line. "What are you up to?"

I smiled so wide it made my cheeks hurt. "I just finished my shift at the library, and I'm about to drive home. What about you? Working hard or hardly working?"

"Well, I was working hard. I'm about to head into some meetings for the rest of the day, but I wanted to call and hear your voice."

I was too stunned to even speak.

When had Don ever called just to hear my voice?

"Pam? You still there?" Alistair asked.

"I'm here, sorry. Just spaced out for a second."

Another laugh. "Happens to me all the time. Do you want to do dinner tonight?"

With the two-hour time difference, our version of a dinner date was Alistair video chatting me from his office while he finished up with work, and I cooked myself dinner. The first time we'd done it, I'd felt a little awkward, like I was hosting a cooking show or something, but now it was something in my day I looked forward to.

"I'd love that. I hope your meetings aren't too painful." I didn't know much about conducting business at the level Alistair did, but from what he'd told me, most of his meetings could have been an email.

"They won't be now that I have this to look forward to. I'll talk to you later, babe."

Babe.

My brain tingled every time he called me that in his rumbly voice.

"Talk to you then, bye."

I TRUST MY PATH.
   I embrace change.
   I am worthy of love.

THOSE WERE JUST a few of the affirmations I'd scribbled down from the book.

Whatever preconceived notions I had about *Finding Yourself After Forty: How Mantras, Meditation, and Daily Yoga Transformed My Life* were wrong. Keeping good on my promise to Nancy, I'd dug into the book as soon as I got home from the library. For the past few hours, I'd been enamored with the author, Jane Stone's, story.

She'd spent most of her life as a stay-at-home mom, and when her husband passed, she felt lost—until a friend introduced her to yoga. Through her yoga practice, mantras, and affirmations, she transformed her mindset and found a sense of purpose.

It was relatable—almost like this book was written for me.

"Shit," I said under my breath when Alistair's video chat request came through. I'd been so engrossed with the book that I'd lost track of time.

"There she is," he said when I answered. "What are you up to, pretty lady?"

Alistair's smiling face filled my screen. Today he was

dressed in a baby blue button-down shirt that comple-mented his cream-colored hair, the neck unbuttoned just enough that the wispy grays of his chest hair peeked out.

I propped my phone against the vase on my kitchen table and pushed my glasses up my nose. "I was reading and lost track of time. It's probably a sandwich for dinner type of night."

"What were you reading?" He lowered his voice. "Does it involve aliens?"

I loved that he was interested and genuinely wanted to know—even if he assumed it was smut.

"No," I said with a laugh. "No aliens in this one. My friend recommended this book about mantras and yoga. I thought it would be super crunchy, but it's really inspiring. The author changed her entire life because she believed she could. I mean, I'm sure there's more to it than that, but a lot of the affirmations she mentions resonate with me."

He rubbed the scraggly whiskers dotting his chin. "There are a lot of successful people who believe in the power of affirmations. It's a pretty common theme in the business books I've read."

"Do you think it actually works?" I asked in a low whisper.

Alistair thought for a moment, then slowly nodded his head. "I do. If you put those vibes out into the universe, I believe it answers."

I snorted. "Did you eat an edible before you called?" I knew the answer was no because he still had to drive home, but it was the type of profound statement you'd expect from someone under the influence of marijuana.

"No," he laughed. "It's just in the air here all the time. We live in a marijuana cloud. Seriously though..." Alistair put his arms on his desk and leaned in closer, his expression softening. "I think that if you're interested in the techniques she mentions in the book, you should give it a try. Write your mantras down and will those things into existence. Hell, maybe even sign up for a yoga class. I've been thinking of taking it up myself. You saw me on the ice! Gotta work on my balance."

So this was what it was like to date someone who was supportive.

If I had mentioned something like affirmations or yoga to Don, he would have laughed in my face.

But that wasn't the case now.

I looked at Alistair and grinned. "You know, I think I will."

TWELVE

ALISTAIR

"What seems to us as bitter trials are often blessings in disguise." - Oscar Wilde

---

Another fucking meeting.

When you were this high up the corporate ladder, it's what the majority of your workday consisted of. Luckily, my business partner Jonathan insisted on leading the meeting. The minotaur was ten years my junior, and he was slowly taking on more responsibilities at Rocky Roots Cannabis Corporation, the company we'd spent the last seven years building from the ground up.

I leaned back in my chair, watching Jonathan advance the slideshow he'd prepared. The social media profile of an attractive, sun-kissed blonde with a joint hanging out of her mouth appeared on the screen, boasting an impressive 1.3 million followers on the platform.

Yet I had no clue who she was.

"The last item on today's agenda is the influencer social

media campaign. We've already had an impressive number of influencers sign on—"

I cut in. "I thought we decided to table that idea so we could test organic promotion before moving forward with paid."

"Well." Jonathan sucked his teeth. "The majority voted to pursue this paid strategy to increase revenue this quarter."

I understood that, but in my mind, that money could be used for raises for our pickers and factory workers—the people who were the backbone of this company. What happened to the days when it was enough to send a box of swag and a bunch of free rolling papers?

Was I really that out of touch?

"Alright, then. If we think it'll increase revenue," I said with a sigh. "Must have missed the memo on that while I was gone."

"Don't worry, Al. Change is scary, but this will really benefit the company." He walked around the table, stopping behind me and clasping one of his hands on my shoulder. "We'll do lunch soon, and I'll bring you up to speed on everything."

What in the actual fuck?

Who was this condescending prick, and what had he done with Jonathan?

I seethed through the rest of the meeting, letting each word that came out of Jonathan's mouth go in one ear and out the other. Instead of making small talk with everyone on the board or joining them for lunch, I retreated to my office, slamming the door shut behind me as I went.

"That motherfucker," I hissed and plopped down in my chair.

Was this some sort of power play? I thought that alpha male posturing had gone out of style.

As I massaged the base of my ears and contemplated my choice in business partners, and hell, my life in general, my phone vibrated with a text message.

It was like she knew I needed something to pull me out of my funk.

> Pam: Look what I did today!

She followed the message with a picture of her Leviathan Fitness membership card. Her smiling face beamed at the camera, her glasses catching the glare from the flash. She was so beautiful, and even though she couldn't see me, I couldn't help but smile back.

> Me: Look at you, pretty lady! When's your first class?

I was glad Pam had taken this step. I wanted her to pursue anything that interested her, to do something for herself. It's hard prioritizing yourself when you're a parent, but now that her kids were grown and Don wasn't around, there was nothing holding her back except her own self-perceived limits.

While I waited for her to respond, a phone call notification flashed over the screen.

Chai.

My daughter rarely called me, preferring text messages to keep in touch.

Fuck.

Was everything alright?

"Hey, kid. Everything alright?" I asked, my pulse

hammering. I was doing my best to steel my emotions and seem chill, but there was still a slight tremble in my voice.

She sighed, the same 'I'm sick of you worrying about me' sigh she'd given me for the past few months. "Dad. Can you stop? I'm fine. I called to tell you something exciting, and you totally killed my vibe."

Could I stop?

When you had a kid, there was no stopping. It was like a piece of your heart lived outside of your chest. No matter how old they were, how far away, you'd always love them fiercely, worrying about them until you took your last breath.

"Alright, alright," I huffed. "I'm sorry for killing the vibe. What's up?"

"I just met Pam," she said slyly.

"No shit. I was just texting her. Were you working the desk?"

"Actually, Atlas introduced us because I'm teaching the beginner yoga class she signed up for."

"Why are you teaching the beginner yoga class?"

Chai normally worked the front desk and had her own personal training clients. She had experience with yoga, but I'd never known her to teach any classes...

"Our normal instructor is really busy with her own studio, and I wanted to make a little extra money, so I told Atlas I would—"

"Do you need money, hun? You know I'm happy to help you. The past few months have been a lot for you." I hated the idea of her struggling, especially when I had more money than I knew what to do with.

She let out an exasperated breath. "Dad, if I really needed help, I'd ask you, but I like being independent. It's not like I'm in dire straits or anything. I'm just trying to make up for the work I missed."

That was my kid. Headstrong and independent. Sometimes I loved it; other times she made me want to rip my hair out.

"Just remember the offer's always there, kid. I've got your back."

"I know, Dad. I never doubted that for a second."

I grinned, feeling like this was one of those parenting wins. "So, what did you think about Pam?"

I was dying to know her thoughts. After all, she was the one who encouraged me to start dating again. Chai had zero hang-ups when it came to my relationship with her mother. We'd been divorced for so long that she'd never harbored any negative feelings toward anyone new I brought into my life—unless it was deserved.

"She is freaking precious. I mean, I figured she was going to be a total sweetheart because Tegan is, but Reece is also her kid..."

"Is he really that bad?" I asked with a laugh. The more I learned about Reece, the more anxious I got about meeting him one day.

"He's a lot better with Cyrus in the picture, but I've heard he was kind of a jerk before that."

What Pam and those photographs told me about Don came to mind. Poor Reece was probably riddled with childhood trauma, and he'd likely dealt with it the unhealthy way a 'man's man' was taught to—by lashing out.

"Well, at least he's working on himself. From what Pam told me, his father wasn't the best role model."

"We can't all have amazing dads."

I laughed, feeling the tension from the meeting slipping away. "You did get pretty lucky, didn't you? But that's enough stroking my ego. Tell me more about the class you're teaching. I want to know what Pam is in for."

"It's Hatha yoga for beginners, so I'll be focusing on poses and breathing exercises. Making sure they have good form. We'll discuss mantras and meditation, so there's a mental health component to it as well."

Mantras.

Since Pam had read that book, mantras and affirmations had become her thing. She'd even texted me one this morning: *I release all negativity from my mind and body.*

It was perfect for the afternoon I'd had.

"She's going to love that. I think she's on a little bit of a journey."

"I hope she does, and I mean, yoga is a healthier coping mechanism than buying a sports car."

"Are you forgetting that we met on a dating app, went on one date, and decided to embark on a long-distance relationship? I think we're both having some sort of crisis."

It was the first time I'd admitted it—but maybe I was. Perhaps this whole thing with Pam and with work was the culmination of my age and loneliness catching up with me.

Chai sighed and I imagined her tail was twitching with annoyance. "Dad, you're not having a crisis. You met, hit it off, and decided to see where things go. And honestly, with the way everything fell into place, the whole thing feels like it might be fate."

"Fate, huh?"

"Even if minotaurs don't have fated mates, the universe works in mysterious ways. I haven't seen you this happy in a long time."

Other than the distance and the tension at work, she was right.

This was the happiest I'd felt in years.

"You're right, kid. I'm probably just overthinking it."

"I am right, and you're totally overthinking it," she said with a laugh. "And you know, in terms of the whole distance thing, you could always move to Briar Glenn."

"Hun, my job—"

Chai interrupted before I could continue with my list of excuses. "Respectfully, fuck that job. You've made your money, Dad. Retire early so you can enjoy it."

I *could* retire early, but then what? Just sell my house and all my shit and move to Briar Glenn?

While the idea of living in the same town as Pam and my daughter was appealing, I wasn't sure I was ready for retirement. I'd spent so much of my life working, pulling long hours, and dedicating myself to the various companies I'd worked for, that I wasn't sure I knew how to just relax. Hell, even the time I spent working remotely while caring for Chai had been tough on me.

"I'll think about it," I said, doing my best to sound convincing.

"Mhmm," she hummed, totally unconvinced. "Well, I've gotta run, Dad. I have a client arriving in a few minutes."

"Alright, baby. Love you."

"Love you, too. Bye."

As soon as we hung up, I got a text message from Pam.

> Pam: Sorry, I was driving! Oh my gods!! I met Chai today! She is so sweet! She's instructing the yoga class I'm taking!

I smiled down at my phone before typing out a message. Her excitement was contagious.

Me: She just called and told me all about it. I'm glad the two most important ladies in my life finally got to meet.

Pam: You're making me blush. How's your day going?

Alistair: Let's just say the mantra you sent me this morning applies to today.

Pam: That bad, huh? Would a dinner date help?

Just the thought of chatting with her while she cooked, watching as she blew her bangs out of her face and held the knife in a way that made me concerned for her fingers, perked me up.

Alistair: I'd never turn down a date with a beautiful woman.

The rest of the day would drag, but at least now, I had something to look forward to.

THIRTEEN

PAM

I love what my body is capable of doing.

I squatted in front of my affirmation-lined mirror—well, as far as my knees would allow me to squat—ensuring my butt wasn't visible through my tight black leggings. Tegan had assured me they were fine, and the tag had claimed "squat-proof," but I wasn't willing to risk it when I would be bending over right in front of a stranger.

Should I wear underwear?

I mean, I did with normal leggings. It had taken years for me to overcome the damage of the anti-panty line craze of the 80s and 90s, *but now*, you'd have to pry my full-coverage cotton briefs from my cold, dead hands.

And besides, if my crotch or butt got sweaty or I had a little leak, it would be an additional layer of absorbency.

Fully convinced, I peeled the leggings off and strutted over to my dresser. The second my fingers made contact with a comfy pair of granny panties, I heard my phone vibrate with a text message.

A smile stretched over my face because I was pretty certain I knew who it was from. Still clutching my panties, I retrieved my phone from the bathroom counter, and sure enough—it was a text from Alistair.

> Alistair: Hey pretty lady, getting ready for yoga?

> Me: Yep, getting dressed now.

> Alistair: Getting dressed? I wish I was there to see that.

I wished he was, too. I missed him more each day. Every phone call, dinner date, late night conversation, and good morning text message made being apart that much harder. Other than the distance, things with Alistair were perfect.

A perfect gentleman, a perfect kisser—not to mention his skills in the bedroom.

When would we get to do that again?

Sure, we were dating, but it had its limits.

But did it have to?

I pulled on my underwear and typed out a response.

> Me: I can send you a picture if you want 😉

> Alistair: Pamela Rollins. Are you going to send me nudes?

I slapped my hand over my eyes and snorted. I wasn't quite ready to send him nude pictures, but my underwear and yoga tank were the equivalent of a bathing suit.

That I could do.

> Me: Would a picture of me in my underwear suffice?

> Alistair: Sweetheart, I'm happy with whatever you give me. It could be a picture of your smiling face and I'd still be thrilled.

I couldn't believe this was my life. How did I get lucky enough to have a minotaur plucked from the pages of a romance novel and tossed into my life? These things didn't happen to me—but this *was* my life, and it was about time I started to live it.

I walked in front of the mirror, adjusted my bun, and fluffed my bangs with my fingers.

How did you pose for these types of pictures?

I put my hand on my waist and cocked my hip, the roll of my love handles peeking out from underneath my tank. Giving the mirror the most sensual look I could, I snapped the picture.

Damn, I looked good.

That was one thing that had come with age—confidence in my body. Every wrinkle, stretch mark, and scar told a story. My body wasn't the same as when I was twenty, or even forty, but I loved it all the same.

I sent it over to Alistair, and his response was almost immediate.

> Alistair: Holy Goddess, woman 😍. I wish those thighs were hugging my face.

Shit.

I clenched my legs together, remembering how good he'd made me feel. Not just good, but cherished, because my pleasure was important to him.

Me: I wish they were too.

Alistair: The things I'd do to you…

A few suggestive text messages and I could already feel myself getting wet. In fifteen minutes, I'd be taking my first yoga class.

Instructed by his daughter.

There was no way I could do this right now.

Me: As much as I'm enjoying this, I have a yoga class in 15 minutes, and your daughter is the instructor.

Alistair: 😬 You're right, you're right. But can we continue this conversation another time??

Me: I'd like that very much. I'll text you after class!

Ten minutes later, I rushed out of my house and hopped in my car. Normally, I walked to the businesses along Main Street, but with the little distraction I'd experienced before I left, there wasn't enough time for that. I didn't want to be late for my first class, especially when Alistair's daughter was the instructor. Creeping in after things already started would be embarrassing—and what if Chai locked the door once class started…

With just a few minutes to spare, I pulled into the parking lot of Leviathan Fitness. I grabbed my yoga mat and water bottle from the passenger seat and booked it to the gym doors.

"Hey there, Mrs. Rollins," Fallon said from behind the

front desk. "Lookin good!" He clicked his beak and gave me a wink of one of his beady bird eyes.

"Thank you, Fallon. I'm running a little late for the beginner yoga class. Can you show me to the studio?"

"Absolutely. Follow me."

Walking on all fours, he stepped out from behind the desk and led me down a hallway lined with doors. One of them was slightly ajar, and I could hear Atlas' gruff voice coming from inside. I made a mental note to say hello to him once my class was finished.

"I gotta get back to the desk, but just follow the hallway straight back," Fallon chirped, his tail swishing behind him as he strutted off.

At the end of the hallway, Chai leaned against the door-frame, waiting to greet the attendees.

"Hey, Mrs. Rollins," Chai said when she caught sight of me.

"Please, call me Pam."

Chai gave me a kind smile that reminded me of her father. "How are you feeling today, Pam?"

I gripped my yoga mat tight, feeling unnerved by her presence and the fact that I was doing something new. "I'm a little nervous."

"Everyone's nervous before their first class, but I promise you'll feel great once everything is said and done. Do you have any injuries I should know about?"

I thought for a second, going over the aches and pains I'd been experiencing lately. "I have some arthritis in my knees, and I've been known to tweak my back occasionally. My flexibility isn't great, but I'm hoping yoga improves that."

She nodded, her considerably smaller horns bobbing up and down. "Alright. I'll keep an eye on you and suggest modifications as needed." Chai held up a round piece of plastic. "This is a consent token. The green side is labeled with 'yes' to let me know you're okay with me making hands-on form adjustments, and the red side is labeled with 'no' to let me know you'd prefer verbal adjustments. Just go with whatever you're comfortable with, okay?"

Well, I loved that.

Even though I was comfortable with hands-on adjustments, it was nice to know consent was important—especially without having to ask.

"Okay," I said and took the token from her.

"You can head inside and set your mat up wherever you want. Once you've done that, grab two blocks and a yoga strap from the rack. You can sit and relax or meditate until the class begins."

I inhaled deeply and nodded. "Alright."

"It's going to be great."

Chai stepped out of the doorway, and I slipped inside the studio. Calming music filled the space, with several humans and monsters sitting crossed-legged on their mats with their eyes closed, waiting for the class to begin. Since Briar Glenn was such a small town, I expected to see some familiar faces but didn't recognize a soul. It was comforting in a way. If I embarrassed myself, at least it would be in front of strangers.

Strangers and my boyfriend's daughter.

No pressure, Pam.

I hung up my coat and tucked my shoes into one of the cubbies that lined the back wall. After spreading out my mat in a part of the room that gave me plenty of space to switch positions, I grabbed my blocks and strap. With my token 'yes' side up—and with some difficulty—I sat cross-legged in the center of my mat.

Closing my eyes, I focused on the music. The droning sound of the singing bowl started in my head, then drifted down my body, then out through my fingertips and toes. Soft chimes grounded me in the present, and I felt my anxiety slipping away.

A clacking that I assumed was the sound of Chai's hooves against the wooden floor joined the music as she walked around the room.

"Hello and good morning," she said calmly. "My name is Chai, and I'll be guiding you through your practice for the next hour. We'll begin lying down, so please start to make yourself comfortable. Tuck your shoulder blades under your back and let your arms splay out with your palms up. Let your legs spread out to the corners of your mat, and let your ankles roll to whatever position feels natural. If lying with your legs straight out is uncomfortable, bend your knees and place the soles of your feet flat on the mat."

There was a shuffling of bodies as everyone assumed the position that was most comfortable to them. I placed my legs straight out, allowing my ankles to roll outward and feeling a nice stretch through my body.

"Excellent," Chai praised. "Close your eyes and turn your focus inward. Let go of anything happening outside of this space. Let go of any stress or anxiety you might be feeling. Bring your focus to the present moment. It's normal for outside thoughts to pop up during your practice. Take a moment to acknowledge those thoughts, then send them away from you when you exhale. Just let them go."

Chai guided the class through meditation and then stretching for several minutes, instructing us on breathing techniques, and stressed the idea of proper form over depth during poses.

"Now that we're warmed up, we'll move into our first

asana, or pose." Chai moved so that she sat on her knees with her hooves pointed out behind her—and the class followed suit. I felt a slight stretch along the sides of my knees, but it wasn't anything painful.

"*Balasana* is Sanskrit for child's pose," she continued once she had everyone's attention. "We'll be learning the Sanskrit names throughout our sessions. We're going to take a deep breath in through our nose, then exhale while we lean forward. Stretching your arms outward, bring your palms to the mat, lengthening your spine."

I watched Chai, studying each of her controlled movements as she performed the pose. She made it look so fluid, *so effortless*. Meanwhile, I felt rigid and out of practice—but that's what I was here for.

Inhaling deeply, I leaned forward as I exhaled, letting my wandering thoughts and negativity leave me with the pose.

While my head was down and I held the asana, Chai spoke again. "Listen to your body. Know that whatever you do is perfect. Don't compare yourself or your body to anyone else. Do what's right for your body and honor yourself with your yoga practice. Let's move into our next asana."

———

BY THE END OF CLASS, my mind was calm and at ease, and my body felt loose and relaxed. I was positive I'd be sore tomorrow, but it would be the good kind of sore that came along with moving your body.

We wiped down our mats and returned our equipment to the racks, the other students making conversation before filing out the door. I packed my things slowly, dragging it out until Chai and I were the only ones left in the studio.

"So what did you think?" she asked with a smile.

I took a deep breath. "You know, I really enjoyed it. It was nice to let go of my thoughts and focus on my body and my breathing. Some of the asanas were a little difficult, but I'm sure it'll get easier as my flexibility improves."

Her ears perked up. "I take it you'll be at the next class?"

"Yeah," I said with a nod, not needing time to think about it. "I will."

She clasped her hands together and bounced from hoof to hoof. "I'm so glad! And it'll absolutely get easier over time. We're striving for progress, not perfection."

Progress, not perfection.

That was another one for my mirror.

FOURTEEN

ALISTAIR

February

This too shall pass.

A loud crack echoed over the mountainside as the axe collided with the log, splintering it into pieces.

"Still got it," I said with a smile.

After wiping the sweat from where it collected along my hairy brow, I tossed the pieces of firewood into the wheelbarrow. Even though it was a crisp forty-five degrees out, chopping wood still made me work up a sweat.

Yeah, I had a log splitter. But every once in a while, when I was feeling myself, I liked to play the role of lumberjack. And with Pam in my life, I was feeling myself a lot lately.

I chuckled under my breath, reminded of those books she read about the mountain men who had a breeding kink.

While I didn't live in Montana, and we were well past our baby-making prime, I wouldn't mind practicing.

Pam and I were a little over a month into things, and I was really starting to feel the distance. Phone calls, text messages, video chats. I couldn't get enough of her. Every day I came home to an empty, joyless house from a job I was feeling increasingly detached from.

She was the highlight of my day.

Hell, maybe even my life.

But did she feel the same?

Was it too soon?

It had to be too soon.

With a heavy sigh, I pushed the wheelbarrow into the garage and mentally prepared myself to carry all the fucking firewood inside.

Maybe I should take an edible first.

Put some music on and let myself mellow out before doing the part of lumberjacking that I despised.

I laughed at myself again.

Lumberjacking.

I'd have to ask Pam if the series used that term. If not, it was a missed opportunity.

I gave my hooves a quick wipe with the towel I kept hanging in the garage, then clopped up the wooden steps and across the polished concrete that covered the ground floor. I scanned my record collection, hoping to find something with a steady beat that would allow me to find a groove while performing this monotonous task.

There was only one band who would do the trick.

Led Zeppelin.

While I had a lot of original pressings that I'd hunted down over the years—and paid an extravagant amount of money for—I decided on a more recent compilation record of the band's greatest hits.

Robert Plant's voice bellowed from the surround sound, the noise bouncing off of the concrete and echoing throughout the house. It was loud, it was rock and roll. It was just how I liked it.

Bopping my horns to the beat of the music, I rummaged through the stash drawer in my kitchen, trying to figure out what I was in the mood for. When you worked for a cannabis company, these things were infinitely more difficult.

What concentration of THC did I want?

Which strain?

What ratio of THC to CBD?

I had as many options as a dispensary.

Ultimately, I decided to go with something middle-of-the-road. I had things to do—and I didn't want to zonk myself out and miss a text or phone call from Pam.

I popped the gummy into my mouth, giving it a good chew before I swallowed it.

Shit.

Regardless of the formula, they all had that funky weed aftertaste.

With about thirty minutes to kill until the edible kicked in, I threw myself onto the couch with my hooves propped over the armrest and checked the time on my phone. Factoring in the time difference, Pam should be finishing up her yoga class any time now—meaning she would hopefully give me a call not long after that.

I opened up our text conversation and scrolled to the screen where I could see all the pictures we'd exchanged over the past month. I'd sent her photos of beautiful mountain sunrises, my deck coated in a heavy layer of snow, and some self-indulgent selfies with my chest hair showing—just because I knew she liked it.

In return, she'd sent me pictures of Remi, her progress on her knitting projects, and of course, some selfies. The one of her in her underwear nearly killed me.

How was it that a woman like her had a husband who never went down on her? Never treated her the way she deserved to be treated?

"Fuck," I groaned and rubbed my temples.

I was head over hooves for her.

My phone vibrated with an incoming call from Pam, and I almost dropped it on my face.

"Hey, pretty lady. How did you know I was thinking about you?" I asked as suavely as I possibly could.

"Stop it," she said with a laugh. "You know I look like a hot mess after yoga."

"That's a lie. You never look like a hot mess, at least not to me."

It brought to mind how she'd looked after we had sex. Her face flushed, her body nice and relaxed. Even when she was sweaty and exhausted, I still thought she was beautiful.

"You're my boyfriend," she huffed. "Of course, you're going to say that."

Her boyfriend.

My heart pitter-pattered every time she called me that, like we were a couple of kids or something.

I grinned. "Even if I wasn't, I'd still think that. How was yoga?"

"It was amazing. Chai really is a great instructor. My flexibility and my headspace are already improving. It's nice to just focus on my breathing and let everything else go— even if it's only for an hour."

Chai had already called me several times, telling me

how much Pam seemed to enjoy the class and how much she'd improved, but I loved hearing it from Pam. There was a sense of passion and excitement whenever she brought up affirmations or yoga.

"That's great, babe. I'm still so proud of you for doing something for *you*. Most folks are so stuck in their ways that they never try new things."

Online dating, a long-distance relationship, yoga. Pam was really out there doing the damn thing. I was lucky enough to be a part of it.

But I could be an even bigger part of it.

I switched the call to speakerphone, searched my online shopping app for a complete yoga set, and hit the 'buy now' button on the first kit with decent reviews.

"Thank you for encouraging me. I don't think I would have followed through with any of this if it wasn't for you. Don would have told me I was crazy."

I cringed every time she mentioned Don—and not out of jealousy. It was because he sounded like a total dick.

"I'll always support you in anything you want to do. Speaking of *doing things*, when are you going to fly out here and visit me?"

She was quiet for a second. "You know I'm afraid of flying."

My mouth gaped open. "You're afraid of flying? How in the hell have we never talked about this?"

"I told you I've never left Briar Glenn!"

"Yeah, but you didn't mention that it was because you're afraid of flying," I huffed.

How in the ever-loving fuck was I going to get her out here to visit if she was afraid of flying?

"I mean, I didn't start out with that fear, but as the years passed and I never had the opportunity to get on a plane, it just sort of intensified. I've seen too many movies about plane crashes."

"So I guess that means you're never going to make it out here to visit me," I said with a sigh.

Pam was quiet again, obviously giving it some thought. "I mean, for you, I'd consider it. No guarantees I wouldn't chicken out at the gate, though."

One corner of my lips tugged up ever so slightly. "At least that isn't a no."

"I can't ever imagine telling you no, Alistair Reid."

"Ha! Am I really that charming?"

"Maybe," she mumbled under her breath.

"I—uh." I cleared my throat, feeling the effects of my edible and debating if I should just put it all out there. "I really miss you, Pam."

"I miss you, too," she said without missing a beat.

I could hear the sadness in her voice. What started as a happy conversation went south within a matter of minutes. The distance, Pam's fear of flying, everything hit us all at once.

We were both quiet, with nothing but Zeppelin filling the silence between us.

"I should probably get going. There's snow in the forecast, and I wanna get this firewood in the house before it starts falling." It was a bullshit excuse, but I needed a few minutes alone to process things.

"Oh, okay," she said quietly. "Well, I'll be around later if you want to video chat. I'd love to see that handsome face of yours."

Fuck. I'd obviously upset her.

"I'd like to see you too, sweetheart. I'll give you a call a little bit later, okay?" Lugging the wood inside the house and letting this edible settle in would give me the time I needed to think about this.

"Alright. Talk to you later."

"Bye."

Motherfucker.

What was I doing with my life?

Oh right, I was falling for a woman who lived halfway across the country.

I rose from the couch with a groan and headed out to the garage. The whole long-distance thing was working for now, but the closer I got to Pam, the harder it was to do this. I wanted her in my life.

I wanted to be with her.

She was doing some soul searching. I guessed it was about time I did some, too.

FIFTEEN

PAM

I surround myself with loving people.

No matter what I did, I couldn't stop dwelling on the conversation I had with Alistair the other day. Knitting, romance novels, yoga—none of it distracted me from the fact that the distance between us was a limiting factor in our relationship. Well, that and my fear of flying.

After sacrificing so much of myself during my marriage, was I wrong in committing to the first person I met after putting myself out there? Alistair and I had only been on one date. He was my first dip into the dating pool, and I jumped right into a relationship with him—and a long-distance one at that.

His dick and the multiple orgasms he gave me must have clouded my judgment—or at least influenced my decision.

"Ma!" Reece shouted, causing me to jump. "I asked you a question."

I was at brunch with Reece and Cyrus this morning, but I was having a hard time being present.

I pushed my glasses up my nose and gave my son a polite smile. "Sorry, honey. What was the question, again?"

Reece sighed and I caught Cyrus giving him a look. "I just wanted to know how things were going with that Alistair guy. You've seemed kind of—I don't know—absent. Sort of like right now."

"What do you mean?" I tilted my head in confusion.

"Come on, squish. Help me out here," Reece grumbled under his breath.

Cyrus cleared his throat, his tentacle wrapping around Reece's forearm. "I think what Reece is trying to say is that you've been a little more withdrawn since you started to date Alistair. He—*we*—don't want you to feel like you can't talk to us about him."

"I promise you, I don't think it's weird or anything. Maybe the long-distance thing is a little weird, but I'm glad you're seeing someone." Reece leaned over the table slightly, lowering his voice to keep what he was saying between the three of us. "I want you to be happy, Ma. I always thought you deserved more than what Dad gave you, and deep down, you knew that, too."

It was enough to bring tears to my eyes.

As prickly as my son could be, he was pretty perceptive —especially when it came to his mama. I had been a little withdrawn, not just because of any weirdness I felt about dating again but because Alistair and yoga took up most of my time these days. To put it bluntly, I wasn't up my kids' asses like I used to be. It was an adjustment for them as much as it was for me.

I took off my glasses and dabbed at my eyes with a napkin. "I appreciate that, honey. I've just been busy with yoga and the library—and I give Alistair a lot of my free time now. I'm sorry if I've been distant."

"Aw, Ma. Don't cry." Reece reached across the table and grabbed my hand. "We miss you, but we want you to have all the happiness in the world."

Cyrus nodded his head in agreement.

"Cyrus is really rubbing off on you," I told Reece with a laugh.

His cheeks flushed, and he pursed his mustache down over his lip. "I'm comfortable enough with my masculinity to talk about my feelings."

"You're doing great, darling," Cyrus whispered and planted a kiss on Reece's cheek, deepening his blush.

They were so stinking cute together. Such an unlikely couple but a perfect match nonetheless.

"Now that we've got that out of the way," Reece said, "when are you going to visit him? Or when is he coming back here?"

"You know I'm afraid of flying." I sighed, not excited to discuss the topic that had been plaguing me for the past week.

"There are medications to help with that," Cyrus said with a wide grin that showed off the sharp tips of his teeth. "They mellow you out a bit, and the next thing you know, you'll have landed in Colorado."

"Yep." Reece nodded. "I got some from my doctor for our trip to England, and that's a much longer flight."

Maybe with medication, I could do it.

What was that affirmation again...

I can do hard things.

"I'll think about it," I said, and saw Reece give Cyrus a knowing look.

"Where is our waitress?" Cyrus scanned the restaurant for our server. "I don't want Beau to mess in his kennel."

Reece grinned and gripped his hand. "You're such a cute dog dad."

"What can I say? The little furball has grown on me," Cyrus said with a shrug.

I didn't have anywhere to be, and I planned to treat the two of them anyway...

"Why don't you two go take care of Beau, and I'll get the check. I'm not in any rush."

"Mrs. Rollins, we—" Cyrus started, but I cut him off.

"None of that 'Mrs. Rollins' nonsense. I know you're older than me, but it's either Mom or Pam. Mrs. Rollins was Don's mother," I huffed.

Reece pulled out his wallet and threw a few bills on the table. "Let us get the tip then."

I sighed, wishing my son wasn't such a stubborn ass but appreciating the gesture all the same. "If you insist."

They rose from their chairs and came over to say goodbye.

"Thanks, Ma. Love you," Reece said, giving me a tight hug and a kiss on the cheek.

"Love you too, honey."

When it was Cyrus' turn, he gingerly wrapped his arms around me and I squeezed him tight in response.

"Thanks," he grated out before adding, "Mom."

"Aww," I squealed as I pulled away.

It felt like a major victory. We were a family, and Cyrus was a part of it.

I watched them leave, then pulled out my phone to

check for any messages from Alistair while I waited for the check.

I'd told him my plans for the day, and he'd texted me to check-in.

> Alistair: How is brunch going, pretty lady?

I could picture his face, that lopsided smile beaming just like it did each time he called me that.

> Me: I just said goodbye to the boys.
> Waiting for the check now.

> Alistair: When will you be home?

> Me: In about 10 minutes. Why?

> Alistair: I was just thinking about you and how badly I want to kiss every inch of your body. How good I want to make you feel.

A photo came through. A photo of the very impressive swell of Alistair's cock straining against his underwear.

Well that was unexpected.

Hot, but unexpected.

I bit my lip and glanced around the restaurant, paranoid that people would know exactly what I was up to. In reality, no one was paying attention.

> Me: I'll videochat you as soon as I get home.

A video came through next, one of Alistair massaging his cock through the thin material. A wet spot had already formed right where the tip of his cock was.

Alistair: Can't wait.

"Sorry for the wait, Ma'am," the waitress said, and I jumped, fumbling my phone screen-down in my lap.

"Oh, it's fine," I rushed out with a wave of my hand.

Without looking at the check, I handed her my debit card. I didn't care what it cost. I just wanted to get out of there and call Alistair.

She flashed me a strained smile. "I'll be right back with this..."

I SPED HOME, completely disregarding the twenty-five miles-per-hour speed limit signs posted along Briar Glenn's residential streets.

Freaking Alistair Reid. Sending me dirty messages like that.

I hadn't been this horny in years.

Rushing through the door, I gave Remi a little pat and dashed up the stairs—nearly tripping over my feet on the way to my bedroom.

I dropped my coat and purse on the floor in a heap, then climbed into bed with my phone in hand.

How was this going to work?

I didn't have a laptop, so maybe just good old-fashioned phone sex? I was pretty sure Alistair would want to see what I was doing, though...

Oh! My tablet!

I grabbed it from my nightstand and initiated a video chat with Alistair—who answered on the second ring, obviously anticipating the call.

"Hey, beautiful," he said, his voice low and husky. He

was shirtless, that perfect hairy dad bod on display while he lounged against a pile of pillows.

"Hi there."

Alistair repositioned himself, giving me a better view of his body. He wasn't just shirtless—he was naked, with nothing but a thin sheet covering his lower half.

My eyes snapped to the bulge of his cock, and my tongue darted out to wet my lips.

"See something you like?" he asked with a sensual laugh.

I nodded. "Mhmm."

"I want you to do what I ask. Think you can handle that, sweetheart?"

Holy shit.

He was some sort of reincarnated sex god. I was sure of it.

"I think I can handle that."

"Get off the bed."

I moved slowly, doing my best to seem calm and collected, but on the inside, my heart was pounding.

I wanted to feel him, fuck him, please him. Scream his name. Take his cock and his cum again and again. He was in charge, and I enjoyed being at his mercy.

Standing in front of my tablet, I awaited his next instruction.

Alistair smirked and smoothed his thumb over his lip, drawing out the silence between us. "Undress. I want all of it off."

Fuck. Fuck. Fuck.

I shimmed out of my jeans, taking my underwear with them, then pulled my sweater over my head.

"Gods damn," he groaned at the sight of me in nothing

but my bra. His hand traveled down his stomach and disappeared beneath the sheet.

Even with the red lines streaked around my waist from my tight jeans, the pooch of my stomach—Alistair still found me attractive. He could have anyone he wanted, and despite the distance and the difficulties that came along with it, he chose me over anyone else.

To him, *I was worth it.*

And I was finally starting to believe that myself.

He stared at me intently, waiting for me to comply and ruffling the sheet with what I assumed were slow strokes of his cock. I reached behind my back and undid my bra, allowing it to fall to the floor.

"Pam," he breathed. His eyes fluttered closed for a second before snapping open to take me in again.

Being the center of his attention fueled my confidence. Pushing back my shoulders and forcing my chest out, I gave both my nipples a little pinch. Hard enough for me to suck in a breath.

Alistair grinned. "Did that feel good?".

"Yes." But not nearly as good as it would have felt if it were his fingers doing the pinching.

"Get up on the bed."

I leaned in closer, letting my breasts sway in front of the screen. "Where should I set the camera?" I asked coyly.

He bit his lip, his hand moving faster beneath the covers. "Make sure I can see your whole body, like how I have mine."

"You don't want me to set it up between my legs?"

Alastair let out a quiet laugh. "As much as I appreciate that view, I want to see you. All of you, not just that pretty cunt of yours."

Pretty cunt.

I'd always hated the c-word with a passion—until Alastair, that is.

Such filthy words coming out of the mouth of an absolute gentleman did me in.

"Should I grab a toy?" I asked shyly. If I was going to get off without him here, a toy and lube were an absolute necessity.

His smile widened. "Please do. I love playing with toys."

Yep. It was official. I'd won the boyfriend jackpot.

Don had always looked down on using toys, thinking he was a superior lover, but I knew better. His fragile male ego was worried I'd prefer them over him.

Alistair didn't have those insecurities.

"Give me a second." Wrapping my arm around my chest to contain my breasts, I darted out of view and over to my nightstand. Without the proper support, those things were weapons.

Pulling open the second drawer, I perused my collection of dildos, vibrators, and water-based lubes. Old faithful —a classic neon pink rabbit vibrator—was the first to catch my attention. Even though I'd collected some interesting toys since Don's passing, I decided to pick something a little more tame for Alistair.

I grabbed the vibrator and a bottle of lube, then climbed onto the bed. Laying on my side, I mirrored how Alistair was sprawled out in front of the camera, adjusting my tablet so my entire body was in view.

Alistair looked at the vibe and wiggled his eyebrows. "Neon pink. I like it. Can you spread your legs for me a little bit?" he asked.

I nodded and bent my knees, bringing one leg up to give him a better view of my pussy. Spreading myself open like that would have been impossible a couple months ago, but yoga had already improved my flexibility so much.

"Yeah, just like that," Alistair said under his breath. "Lube up your fingers and slip them between your legs. Play with yourself for me. Get your pussy warmed up for your toy."

Snapping open the bottle of lube, I coated my fingers with a generous drop. I ran them along my center, ensuring I was nice and lubricated.

"Fuck," he hissed, his eyes locked on me and his hand moving furiously beneath the sheet.

"When do I get to see you?" I slipped my fingers inside my pussy, a little gasp slipping past my lips.

He chuckled and pulled the sheet away, revealing the thick length of his cock. A shiny bead of precum gathered along the tip, and with a stroke of his hand, he spread it down his shaft.

I was reminded of the way he tasted, the way he filled my mouth and later my pussy with his cum.

Lots and lots of cum.

"What are you thinking about?" he asked.

It was like he knew...

"I was thinking about how you taste. And about how much you cum."

"Mmm. I loved seeing my cum drip out of you," he groaned, the muscles in his forearm flexing as he stroked faster. "Get your toy ready, sweetheart."

I pulled my focus off Alistair long enough to coat my vibrator with a layer of lube. Placing it at my entrance, I waited for his next instruction.

"Go on and start it up. Rub the tip over your clit nice and slow."

The vibrator came to life with a low buzz, and I placed

the wide, rounded bulb against my clit. Gently rubbing it in slow circles, I moaned as the vibrations swept through me.

"How does that feel, sweetheart?"

"Good, but not as good as your mouth," I said, my voice breathy with desire.

I meant it, too. The minotaur had set the bar for pleasure sky high. It wasn't something I'd been able to replicate on my own. I didn't think I'd ever be able to.

"Have I ruined you, Pam Rollins?"

Still rubbing my clit with the vibe, I bit my lip and nodded.

He laughed, obviously pleased. "Lucky for you, beautiful, you've ruined me, too. Now, slip that toy inside and imagine it's me fucking you. That's what you want, isn't it? Me slamming my big cock inside you?"

Fuck.

That's exactly what I wanted, but for now, the rabbit would have to do.

Pushing the vibrator inside of me, I gasped at the stretch and the first wave of vibrations. I started slow, gently rocking my body until the wand rubbed just where I liked it, and the external arm teased my clit.

Alistair stared at me with hooded eyes, his hand wrapped tight around his cock, pumping it with rapid strokes. "Faster, sweetheart. Really fuck yourself with your toy. Show me how you get off when I'm not there to do it for you."

I pulsed the vibrator in and out, hard and fast—just like Alistair had fucked me. With each pass, I edged closer to my orgasm, my moans muffling his heavy breathing.

With my free hand, I licked two fingers, bringing them to my nipple and rubbing tight circles over the hardened peak.

"Such perfect tits," he grunted. His body was getting rigid, his movements growing more erratic with each tight fisted stroke.

My pussy throbbed at the idea of him getting off like this—that despite the distance—I could still make him come.

I drove the vibrator deep, until the internal bulb massaged my cervix, and the external arm pressed down on my clit. The pressure between my legs built, growing tighter, tighter, tighter, until I came undone.

"Alistair," I moaned, fighting to keep my eyes open as my body quivered against the vibrator.

"Pam. Fuck," he rasped with his eyes fixed on me. He jerked his cock faster, his fist colliding with his sheath until his body jolted.

Thick ropes of cum shot out of his cock, again and again, until a puddle formed on the sheet in front of him.

I shut off the vibrator and stared at him with wide eyes.

How had I swallowed all of that without choking on it?

"Shit," he groaned, and tipped his head back. "We should do this more often."

"We should, but don't you need to take care of that?" I asked with a laugh.

He noticed the pool of cum and chuckled. "Good thing I have an industrial strength mattress protector."

I snorted and shook my head. He was too much. "Why don't you get that cleaned up and call me later?"

"Alright, beautiful. I'll talk to you soon."

A grin spread across my face as we ended the call. I snuggled under my blankets, feeling satisfied, but still wishing we didn't live so far apart.

SIXTEEN

ALISTAIR

I can be both afraid and courageous at the same time.

I fucking hated ties.

Tonight I was meeting Jonathan for dinner at some swanky restaurant that required more formal attire than I liked. He'd set this up under the guise that we were 'catching up,' but I knew better. This was our old song and dance. Going out to dinner meant that there was something about the company we needed to discuss. Doing it in a public space forced us to keep our cool. When large sums of money were involved and jobs were on the line, things could get a little intense.

I straightened my tie, combed my hands through my curls, and hopped out of my truck. The valet gave me a look of distaste as I dropped the heavy ring of keys in his palm. In a parking lot full of expensive sports cars, my truck would stick out like a sore thumb.

Buttoning my suit jacket, I strutted into the restaurant with my horns held high. The sooner I got this over with, the sooner I could call Pam. If anyone could soothe my nerves after butting heads with Jonathan, it was her.

Pamela Jean Rollins.

Gods, I missed her.

Some things just weren't the same over video chat, like the way she snorted when she laughed or the little lines that crinkled around the corners of her eyes when she smiled. I couldn't wait to hold her in my arms again. I just wasn't sure when the opportunity to do that would present itself. It was a major bummer that she was afraid of flying.

Pulling out my phone, I sent her a quick text before I reached the hostess station.

> Me: Just got to the restaurant. Can I call you after dinner?

I tapped a hoof on the polished tile, anxiously awaiting her response.

> Pam: Of course. I'm having a little movie marathon with Remi so I'll be up for a while. Try to stay calm and remember: In every moment, peace is a choice.

Shit.

What I wouldn't give to be cuddled on the couch with her and that cat. For now, a phone call would have to suffice.

> Me: Will do, babe. Enjoy the movie!

I tucked my phone into my jacket pocket and

approached the hostess. She was a naga who looked to be around Chai's age and greeted me with a fanged smile.

"Hi," I said and tugged at my tie again. "I'm meeting my business partner for dinner. The reservation should be under Jonathan Milliard."

The hostess tapped on the tablet in front of her, her face illuminated by the screen's glow in the otherwise dim lighting. I was thankful I had tucked a pair of readers in my pocket; otherwise, I wouldn't be able to read the menu.

"Ah yesss," she said, drawing out the word with a hiss . "Mr. Milliard has already arrived. I'll show you to your table."

She grabbed a menu and slithered across the restaurant, leading me through a maze of tables covered with pristine white table clothes. Smooth jazz music accompanied by hushed conversation echoed across the dining room, giving me total elevator vibes—not an elevated dining experience.

We came to a stop where Jonathan was seated at a table for two.

"Alistair," he said with a forced smile and a curt nod.

The prick didn't even get up for a handshake or hug. This had to be serious.

"Here we are," she said, setting my menu down on the table. "Your waiter will be around to take your drink order shortly. Enjoy your meal."

"Thank you." I unbuttoned my jacket and slipped into my seat. "Have you been waiting long?"

"No, not long at all." He took a drink from the rocks glass filled with amber liquor in front of him.

If I had to guess, it was likely whiskey. When we first met, we'd bonded over our shared love for horticulture and our taste for rare whiskeys. Sitting across from him now, we felt more like strangers than business partners.

I leaned back in my chair and ran my thumbs over the tablecloth. "So, how's the family?"

"They're good. Delilah is still getting used to the new baby, but she'll get there. Lauren is absolutely killing it as a mother of two. They really aren't lying when they say it's easier with the second." The corners of his mouth tilted up in a smile, just like they did at every mention of his family.

Gods.

A new baby.

It really drove home that we were at such different points in our lives. He was young, successful, and in the beginning throes of parenthood. I was nearing retirement, had an adult daughter, and was potentially having a mid-life crisis.

"How is Chai doing?" He quickly added, like he just remembered that I had a daughter.

"She's doing much better. Now that she's had surgery, it should be smooth sailing."

"Glad to hear it. I know you were worried there for a bit."

I smiled and shook my head. "You know, no matter how old they are, the worry is always there."

"I guess I'm in for a tough time now that there are two of them," he groaned, and for a second, he reminded me of who he was when we first started the business. The same happy-go-lucky hippie minotaur who wanted to revolutionize Colorado's cannabis industry.

The waiter arrived at the table and took my drink order, whiskey on the rocks, same as Jonathan's.

We made small talk until he returned with my drink, discussing basketball season, podcasts, and the snowy weather we'd been having. We avoided talking about business until I'd made a dent in my drink, and we placed our order, that is.

"Al, I, uh. You probably know why I wanted to meet, don't you?" Leaning over the table, he rubbed his thumb along his jawline.

I straightened in my seat. "Whatever it is, I figured it wasn't great if we're discussing it here. Is this about the meeting the other day and the influencer program?"

He huffed and shook his head. "It isn't about that. I mean, I'm sorry I didn't run it by you, but this isn't about that. I'll cut right to it." Jonathan sat up and puffed out his chest, putting on the same alpha male performance he did at the board meeting. "I want to buy your share of the company."

I tilted my head to the side, my mouth hanging open in disbelief.

Did I hear him right? He wanted to buy me out of the company we'd built from the ground up?

I'd put so much time and energy into Rocky Roots. I was proud of the work we'd done—and he wanted me to just kiss it all goodbye?

"Will you just hear me out?" He pleaded, letting the whole act slip. It was like he was that same young kid with a passion for weed again and not some cutthroat businessman.

I steepled my fingers and stared at him. "I'm listening."

"Al, I care about this company. I have a ton of ideas about how we can grow and reach that next level, but in order to do that, we need to get with the times. The market is changing, and if we don't change with it, we'll be left behind." He took a deep breath. "You've taught me everything I know about this business. If it weren't for you, I'd still be that drug-rug-wearing stoner with a pipe dream. I care about you, Al, and I know you're unhappy here. The stuff with your daughter and whatever else you have going on in your personal life has been a major distraction. I think it's time for you to retire and pass the torch. I know things have been a little tense between us since you returned, but I feel like I've really stepped up."

Those were all valid points, and I would prefer the company stay in the hands of someone who'd been a part of it since its inception—but retirement? I'd thrown the idea around a time or two, especially since Chai got sick and I met Pam, but I wasn't sure I was ready.

"Jonathan, I—I'm not sure I'm ready to make a decision like that just yet. I mean, I'm not even sixty." I ran my hands through my hair and puffed out a breath. When he asked me to dinner, I wasn't expecting *this*.

"Here." Jonathan slid a piece of paper across the table. "This is what I'm prepared to offer."

I slipped on my readers and took in all the zeros that followed the number with wide eyes. There was no way... "Jon, my shares can't possibly be worth this much—"

He could tell by the look on my face that I was in shock. "I discussed it with my financial advisor and my lawyer. It's a fair offer, with a little extra tacked on for everything you've taught me over the years. I know you have savings and a retirement plan, but I want you to live comfortably. You can always invest it into another company if you get bored."

I folded the slip of paper and put it inside my jacket pocket. "Can I have some time to consider your offer?"

"I want you to take some time off. Think it over. Regardless of what you decide to do, I hope this doesn't change things between us."

Even though I was taken off guard, I respected the fact that he'd come to the table with a fair offer.

I had a lot to consider.

It was at that moment that the waiter stopped by the table with our meals. While my couscous looked delicious, I'd suddenly lost my appetite.

THE REMAINDER of the meal was tense. I felt blindsided. Between that and the slip of paper burning a hole in my pocket, I was ready to get out of there.

I gave Jonathan a terse goodbye, and once I hit the highway, I called Pam from my truck's Bluetooth.

It rang and rang and rang again.

"Come on, Pam. Pick up, pick up." I was overwhelmed and I needed to hear her voice.

Her voicemail picked up, but before I could leave her a message, an incoming call from "Pamela Jean" flashed on the screen. I slammed the answer button on the steering wheel.

"Alistair?" she asked, sounding groggy.

Hearing her say my name took my irritation down a notch, and I grinned at the open road in front of me. "Did I wake you, pretty lady?"

"Yeah, but that's okay. How was dinner?"

Where did I even begin?

"Well," I took a deep breath. "Jonathan wants to buy me out of the company."

"And how do you feel about that?" she asked calmly.

"I—I don't even know. I put so much into that company, and I feel like I'm being pushed out—like I'm not keeping up with the times. He even presented me with an offer." I was practically yelling.

"What was his offer?"

I huffed a laugh. "It was a lot of money. A whole lot of money. But I don't need more money, Pam. I'm still young. I've worked my entire life. I don't know anything else but this." My hands tightened around the steering wheel. "He told me to take some time off to think about it."

She was silent for a few seconds, then finally asked, "Do you want me to come out there?"

Fuck.

I wanted that more than anything.

"You're afraid of flying. I would never ask that of you."

"You didn't ask. I offered. I know this is a lot for you to process, and it might be good for you to have some company."

I grinned, practically on the verge of tears. "You'd do that for me?"

She laughed. "I'd do more than that for you. You're gonna owe me big time, though."

I liked the sound of that.

"I'll make it worth your while. I promise. Hell, why don't you bring Remi? He's small enough to fly in the cabin, and he might help you stay calm."

"You wouldn't mind? What about all his—"

"Don't you worry about a thing. Transportation, airfare, I'll take care of it all. You just ensure the two of you make it onto the plane."

"I think I can manage that. Well, with the help of medication, that is." She snorted, and gods, I couldn't wait to hear it in person again.

"I can't wait to see you," I said with a sigh. It meant so much that she was willing to do this for me.

"I can't wait to see you either." She yawned, reminding me just how late it was there.

"I'll let you get some sleep, then tomorrow we'll iron out all the details, okay?"

"Okay. Goodnight, Al."

"Night, sweetheart."

The wheels were already turning. If Pam was willing to get on a plane, I was determined to make it as stress-free as possible.

SEVENTEEN

PAM

I choose to be calm and at peace.

"Okay, Pam. Okay. You can do this," I reminded myself for the umpteenth time this morning. I'd spent the last fifteen minutes pacing back and forth in front of my living room window, waiting for the car that would take me to the airport to arrive.

Both of my kids had offered to drop me off, but Alistair insisted on using some fancy car service with a concierge who would help me with my luggage and make sure I got to where I needed to be.

"I can't believe this is happening," I told Remi.

He let out a miserable meow and clawed at the mesh of his travel carrier as if to say he couldn't believe it was happening either.

Just as the sleek black SUV pulled into the driveway, my phone vibrated with a text message from Alistair.

> Alistair: Your car should be there. Make sure you let the driver help you with your luggage. That's what I'm paying him for.

There was a knock at the door.

That was weird.

Maybe he got notifications from the car service or something.

"Give me just one second," I yelled and typed out a response to Alistair.

> Me: Will do. Can't wait to see you. I'll text you when I make it to the airport.

I opened the front door to find an older gentleman dressed in a black suit that matched the sophistication of the SUV.

"Mrs. Rollins?" he asked.

"Yep. Hi, that's me."

"I'm Ronald. I'll be your driver today. Allow me to help with your bags."

I was only visiting Colorado for a week, but considering the extreme weather, my yoga gear, and the fact that Remi was traveling with me, I'd filled two suitcases to the brim.

Ronald wheeled my suitcases out to the car, and I grabbed Remi and my backpack. Giving my house one last look, I closed the door and locked it behind me.

As I walked to the car, it felt like I was walking on air, which meant the anxiety meds my doctor prescribed were finally kicking in—about time. Ronald opened the door for me, and no sooner had I slipped inside—

"Hey, pretty lady."

That voice.

That deep, rumbly, toe-curling voice.

"No. No!" I said, scrambling further inside. "What are you doing here?" Tears were already threatening my mascara.

Alistair smiled that familiar lopsided grin and held his arms out. After setting Remi down on the seat, I essentially tackled him.

"Oof," he groaned and wrapped his strong arms around me. "You're stronger than you look, you know that?"

I laughed and buried my face in the thick tuft of chest hair peeking out from his shirt. That woodsy sage scent of his felt like home. And my scarf.

He was wearing my scarf.

"You're here," I mumbled.

He nuzzled my temple with his velveteen nose. "Of course, I'm here, babe. There was no way I would let you take your first plane ride by yourself."

Once again, Alistair Reid was like something out of a movie or a romance novel. The type of lover you fantasized about but thought you'd never have. He was like a dream brought to life—and he'd done all of this for me.

Alistair tilted my head up, forcing me to look at him. He was even more handsome than I remembered. "Hey, now. No tears," he said, running his thumb over my cheek.

I snorted, making him grin. "They're happy tears. I missed you so much."

"I missed you too."

He leaned in closer and pressed his lips to mine, his whiskers tickling my face. I opened my mouth for him, savoring the warmth of his breath and the press of his tongue against mine. It was tender at first, the kind of kiss you share when you've been apart from someone and you want to show them just how much you missed them, but it escalated quickly.

"Pam," he groaned into my mouth. That husky voice saying my name was enough to drive me wild.

One of his hands traveled down my chest to gently cup my breast through my sweater, and I melted against him. It felt like an eternity had passed since he'd last touched me. We had a lot of catching up to do.

"Do you want me to touch you?" he asked between kisses.

Fuck.

But the driver.

There was a partition, but I'd never done something so daring. Yet the thought excited me, giving me my answer.

"Please."

He smiled against my lips. "Please, what?"

Always the king of consent, he needed me to say it. Or maybe he *liked* teasing me.

"Please touch me."

His hand slipped over the soft rolls of my stomach, under my sweater, and into my leggings. I was incredibly thankful that I'd chosen comfort over looking cute.

Alistair pushed my underwear to the side, running his fingers through my center while he trailed his lips over my neck.

"You're so wet for me, sweetheart. Do you like the idea of us doing this where someone might hear us and know what we're up to?" I nodded, and he swirled the soft pads of his fingertips over my clit, drawing a gasp out of me that made him chuckle. "My little exhibitionist. What I wouldn't give to fuck you right here."

Slowly, he pushed one finger inside my pussy, pulsing it in and out a few times before adding a second. I arched into him, thrusting my hips into his hand and forcing his fingers deeper.

"You're driving me wild, babe," he whispered, each word a soft graze over my neck. "I can't wait to see you ride my cock like you're riding my fingers."

Shit.

I'd never done that but I'd happily give bull-riding a try if Alistair Reid was between my legs.

He pumped his fingers, adding soft swirls of his thumb over my clit that made my breath hitch.

"Alistair," I moaned, fucking myself against his hand without giving it a second thought. I reached down to massage his cock through his jeans, but he took my wandering hand in his.

"No. There'll be plenty of time for that this week. Right now is all about you, sweetheart. Let me make you feel good."

Well, if he insisted. He loved pleasuring me, and I was more than happy to accept everything he offered.

Alistair curled his fingers, the pads caressing my G-spot with slow strokes while his thumb teased my clit relentlessly. I was getting close, so fucking close, and I had no idea how I was going to stay quiet.

"Gonna come," I stammered.

"You have to be quiet. Can you do that for me?"

"Al—" I whined his name louder than I meant to, and he slipped his hand over my mouth.

"Shh. That's it. Come for me," he whispered in my ear, then nipped on the lobe with his flat teeth, giving it a soft tug.

I shattered, my pussy clenching Alistair's fingers and my moans muffled by his hand clamped tight over my mouth. He worked me through my orgasm, and I vibrated with little jolts of pleasure until his fingers finally stilled. His hand slid from my mouth down to my chin. Forcing me to meet his gaze, he pulled his other hand from my leggings, then put his slick fingers into his mouth, sucking and savoring the taste like I was his favorite dessert.

My lips parted in awe before turning up with a coy smile.

Alistair leaned in until our mouths almost touched, then whispered, "Good. Fucking. Girl."

BECAUSE WE WERE FLYING first class, checking in my luggage and getting through security was a relatively painless process. Initially, I'd felt bad about Alistair springing for a first class ticket, but it made a little more sense now—especially since he was flying with me. If I knew anything about flying economy from the movies I'd seen, it was that space was limited. For a massive minotaur, it just didn't work.

"How are you feeling?" Alistair asked while we were waiting to board.

"Well." I could feel my cheeks getting red. "Thanks to the meds and what happened in the car ride, I'm feeling nice and relaxed."

I couldn't believe I was standing there with him, about to board a plane for the first time in my life.

It was surreal, almost too good to be true, but that's how most things were with Alistair.

There was a ding overhead and the crackle of a microphone. "Group one for the four p.m. flight to Denver is now boarding at Gate C17. Group one for the four p.m. flight to Denver is now boarding at Gate C17. Please have your ticket or cell phone ready."

"That's us, sweetheart. You ready?" he asked, hiking Remi's carrier over his shoulder.

I nodded. "About as ready as I'll ever be." Having him with me made the whole thing much less overwhelming.

The flight attendant smiled at us while she scanned our tickets. "Have a wonderful flight."

We walked down the loading bridge and onto the plane, with Alistair ducking through the doorway to accommodate his horns.

"Here we are," he said, stopping at two cushy lounge seats with plenty of legroom.

"Wow, this is really nice."

He laughed and shook his head. "If you think this is nice, you should see what first class looks like on an international flight."

An international flight.

Nope. Even with Xanax and an orgasm, there was no way I could make it on a flight that long.

The five-hour flight to Denver was enough.

"Why don't you take the window seat."

My face must have given away what I was thinking.

"I promise it's safe. I want you to enjoy the view. When we get closer to Denver, you can really see the Rockies."

"Alright, but if that window busts, you better hold me tight so I don't get sucked out."

"Pamela!" he chuckled, his head swiveling around to make sure no one heard us. "Don't talk about those sorts of things happening!"

Giving him a smug grin, I slipped into my seat. "Am I embarrassing you, the unshakeable and effortlessly cool Alistair Reid?"

Thoughtfully, he tilted his head to the side and gently kissed my forehead. "You could never embarrass me,

Pamela Rollins. I just don't want them siccing the air marshals on us." He took his seat and brought Remi's carrier up to his face. "How ya doin' in there, little buddy? I promise we'll let you out as soon as we get to my place."

Remi responded with a pitiful meow. He really wasn't phased by much, but this was the most time he'd spent in a cat carrier since I'd rescued him two years ago.

Seeing Alistair with him reminded me of how cute they were together. "I'm not sure who you missed more, me or the cat."

"Obviously you, but he's a close second. Stick your bag under here." He set Remi's carrier on the floor and slid it under the seat in front of us, and I did the same with my backpack.

Now that we were seated, the fact that I was about to embark on my first plane ride started to sink in.

I gripped the armrest, my fingers digging into the soft leather.

"Hey," he said, those deep eyes ladened with concern. "Everything is going to be fine."

He placed his hand on top of mine and gave it a tight squeeze, grounding me and quelling some of my anxiety.

"It's nerve-wracking. How much longer until takeoff?"

"It won't be long now. Just gotta wait for everyone else to board, sweetheart." He picked up my hand and placed a soft kiss on my knuckles. "Thank you for doing this for me. It means a lot."

I snorted, and his smile widened. "Oh yes, I'm doing you such a favor when you paid for everything and flew all the way out here to get me."

"It's the thought, though. Of you conquering your fear because I needed to see you."

This time I picked up our hands and kissed his knuckles. "I needed to see you too."

For the first time in a month, it was like we were a real couple. Not that we weren't before, but it made me realize how important a physical connection was.

How had I lived all those years with Don and been indifferent to his touch? With Alistair, I couldn't get enough.

We waited patiently while everyone boarded the plane, with Alistair telling me stories about his various trips to distract me from the impending takeoff.

The sign to fasten your seatbelt flashed, and I clicked mine into place, tightening the belt until it dug into the rolls of my stomach. The stewardess started the safety protocol and I pulled out the brochure to follow along. Alistair looked over at me and shook his head, obviously amused.

At least one of us would know where the emergency doors were located.

As soon as the stewardess sat down, the plane started to move.

"Ready?" Alistair asked with one of his signature lopsided smiles.

"About as ready as I'll ever be," I grated out.

The plane continued down the runway, rattling slightly as it picked up speed.

"Holy goddess," I whispered and clamped my eyes shut, refusing to look as it began to ascend.

"Everything is a-okay. Just the normal takeoff turbulence. Nothing to worry about," he reassured me, his voice calm and even.

From anyone else, it would have been useless, but from Alistair? I believed it.

The rumbling stopped, replaced by an airy, weightless feeling.

"We're up in the air now, Pam," he whispered. "Why don't you open your eyes."

I eased my grip on the armrest, squinting one eye open and then the other. Gazing out the window, I watched as we passed through a thick layer of fluffy clouds and settled in the clear blue sky above them.

"Beautiful," I mumbled with my face pressed against the window.

Alistair leaned over as much as his seatbelt would allow. "This makes it worth it, doesn't it?"

"Maybe, but I'll let you know for sure once we're safely back on the ground."

There was a soft ping, and the stewardess spoke over the intercom. "You may now access your carry-ons. Feel free to connect to the in-flight Wi-Fi, but please keep your devices on airplane mode."

Alistair looked at me and grinned. "Did you bring those earbuds I bought you?"

After Alistair booked my flight, a package of travel essentials mysteriously appeared at my house. A neck pillow, an eye mask, and noise-canceling earbuds.

"Of course I brought them." I pulled out my bag, removing the tiny case that contained the earbuds.

He tapped a few buttons on his phone and pulled out his own earbuds, but instead of bright white, his were sleek black—and considerably larger.

"I got us an audiobook to listen to together." He waggled his eyebrows.

Oh gosh. It was that kind of audiobook. One of my smut books.

Which we were going to listen to on an airplane. Together.

Was I going to join the mile-high club?

There was no way Alistair and I could both fit in an airplane bathroom. With his horns, that would be dangerous.

"You did not. What's it called?"

"I did." He flashed me a smug smile and tilted his phone so I could see the title. "Something about a salacious sex club."

The title.

It finally clicked.

"Is this why you called me a good girl?" I whisper shouted.

He shrugged, his smile growing wider. "*Maybe.* Have you read it?"

I'd heard of it, because who hadn't, but I'd been in such an alien romance chokehold that I'd yet to pick it up.

"No, but I've been meaning to."

"Well, this is perfect then." He leaned in closer. "Now be a good girl and put those earbuds in."

I bit my lip and did as he asked. Suddenly, flying wasn't all that bad.

EIGHTEEN

ALISTAIR

Being romantic is an effortless part of my relationship.

"So what do you think, sweetheart? Was the plane ride worth it?" I asked as my truck climbed up the mountain.

After a fairly uneventful flight and a quick stop at a drive-thru, we were finally on our way to my place.

The sun was just starting to set, coloring the sky above the mountains a blush pink that faded to the deep purple of night.

Pam stared out the window, her gaze fixed on the setting sun. "Of course it was. It's beautiful. And I mean, it was already worth it because I get to see you."

She leaned her head against my shoulder, and gods did I wish that I could hold her hand. Unfortunately, both of mine were preoccupied with the steering wheel. One sharp turn and a patch of black ice could send a vehicle toppling down the mountain. I'd have plenty of time to touch her once we got back to my place; it just wasn't worth the risk.

Remi wailed and scratched at the mesh of his carrier. I felt bad for the poor guy. I was positive he had to pee.

"Don't worry, buddy," I told him. "We're almost there."

I turned down the side road leading to my house, and Pam gasped when it came into view.

"Alistair Reid! How do you live here? It's like something out of a billionaire romance."

I chuckled. "Well, I'm certainly not a billionaire, but I'm glad you like it."

We passed my RV and pulled into the garage. I cut the engine and walked around to open Pam's door for her.

"Thank you." She passed me Remi's carrier, and with my free hand, I helped her down from the truck.

The moment her feet hit the floor, her eyes were scanning the garage walls. I'd covered them in stickers from my travels, using them as an easy-to-carry memento.

"Have you been to all of these places?" she asked in awe.

"Yep. Mostly national parks here in the U.S., but a few are from international trips."

"You've been to so many places, and this was my first time ever flying." Her back was turned, so I couldn't see her expression, but how her voice wavered gave away exactly how she felt.

"Hey," I said, coming up behind her and wrapping my arms around her waist. "Now that you've done it, you can go anywhere you want. I've been to a lot of places, but I haven't been there with you." I spun her around to face me and stared into those bright green eyes. "I am so happy you're here."

"Me too."

"Come on, let's get Remi settled, and I'll grab your luggage in a bit. I want to show you something."

I grabbed her hand, leading her into the house with Remi slung over my shoulder. The moment we stepped inside, she gasped again.

"Alistair! This is beautiful." She ran across the living room to the floor-to-ceiling glass windows that took up an entire wall.

They looked out over the valley, but now that the sun had set, all you could see was a sea of stars. It was the type of view you could only get up here in the mountains. There was no light pollution, no noise from traffic. Just the beauty of nature.

"I can't wait for you to see it in the daylight. Come on, this way."

She joined me, and I led her down the hall to the spare bedroom. A cat tree sat near the window, with a food and water bowl on the floor next to it. Tucked inside the closet was a litter box, and every cat toy known to man was spread out on the bed.

"You did all of this?" she asked, her mouth hanging open.

"I, uh, I wanted to make sure Remi was comfortable here," I said shyly.

Shit.

Maybe I'd gone a little overboard.

Remi scratched at the carrier again, reminding us that he was still confined, and I set him down on the floor. Pam unzipped the top, and, with zero apprehension, the wrinkly little guy jumped out.

"We're here, buddy," she cooed and ran her hand over the portion of his back that wasn't covered by his sweater.

His sweater.

I glanced at Remi and then at Pam.

"Are you wearing matching sweaters?" I asked with a grin.

"Yes," she huffed under her breath and put her hands on her hips. "I have to do something with my extra yarn."

Fuck. She was the most adorable woman I'd ever met.

"You know, I'd like a matching sweater."

She stepped closer, grabbing both sides of the scarf that was still draped over my neck. "I already gave you my favorite scarf, and now you're asking for a sweater."

"Mhmm." I nodded and pressed my forehead against hers.

"Considering you flew out to get me, bought me a first class ticket, listened to a spicy audiobook with me, and did all this for Remi, I think I can do that."

"You know what they say: go big or go home."

"Well, you've certainly got the big part down."

Before I could formulate a response, she tugged on the scarf, pulling my lips to hers. Her body molded into mine, the two of us fitting together like a puzzle piece, and fuck if I didn't feel like she was exactly what my life had been missing.

My hands slid down her sides, over the small of her back, and down to her ass.

Cupping her cheeks, I ground my cock against her body, wishing there wasn't any clothing separating us. Pam whined, all soft and sweet and needy, and just when I thought about lifting her onto the bed and taking her right then and there, a scratching sound came from the closet.

Pam started giggling and pulled away from me.

"Come on, Remi, my man. Such a cockblock," I said with a scowl, making Pam snort.

That snort.

I'd heard it so many times during phone calls and video chats over the past month, but hearing it in person made me smile so wide my cheeks hurt.

"Why don't we give him some privacy and go get your bags? I'll give you a little tour."

"Okay."

I led the way back to the garage and hauled both of her suitcases out of the truck bed. When I grabbed both and started to carry them into the house, Pam stopped me.

"Let me carry one."

I shook my head. "You're my girlfriend, and you're my guest. Besides, with the high altitude, it might be a little tough for you to carry them all the way upstairs..."

She cocked her head. "The altitude?"

"The oxygen pressure is lower up here. It makes you feel a little more out of breath than usual, but the good news is, it should go away in a few days."

"Huh. I thought that was just something that affected the baking instructions for brownies."

"No," I said and shook my head. "It isn't something that only pertains to the cooking times of brownies, but it might throw a wrench in my plan of having you bake something for me while you're here."

She released her grip, letting me carry the suitcases for her, which I considered a small victory.

"With the help of the internet, I'm sure I can still whip something up for you."

We started up the stairs, and after a few moments, I could hear her panting behind me.

"You alright back there?" I asked from over my shoulder.

"You weren't kidding. This is intense. I don't know if I'll be able to do my morning yoga."

I grinned.

So she did plan to continue her practice while she was here.

I couldn't wait to surprise her.

"I think you'll be okay as long as you take deep breaths and don't do any strenuous poses."

"I'm not really doing any strenuous poses yet, but my flexibility and mentality have gotten a lot better."

"I've noticed the shift in your mentality, but I might need a demonstration of your flexibility." I turned and gave her a corny wink that made her giggle.

"Suddenly, the altitude is bothering me a lot less."

This fucking woman. I was glad she wanted it just as much as I did.

"Here we are," I said when we finally reached my bedroom.

It was open and spacious, painted a bright white with dark, exposed wood beams running across the ceiling. A king-size bed sat against a far wall, looking out over the valley through another set of floor-to-ceiling glass windows. I was generally pretty tidy, but I'd had my housekeeper come for a deep clean while I was en route to pick up Pam. When you're a hairy minotaur, the shower could get gross pretty quick.

Pam ran her fingers over the plush blanket at the foot of the bed, one that Chai had given me for Christmas a few years ago. "This is really how it is all the time? You didn't have an interior designer come in and spruce up the place once I said I would visit?"

"You're looking at the interior designer. This is all me, babe."

"What is this?" She grabbed a book off my nightstand, flipping it over to read the blurb.

Shit.

I could have sworn I put that away...

"It's an omegaverse why choose romance. Ever read one of those?"

She put the book down and wrinkled her nose. "Nope. Wolven son-in-law. I just can't bring myself to do it. The same goes for tentacles."

I sighed and shook my head. "Well, that one is ruined for me now."

It wasn't.

It was too good not to finish it.

"Let me show you the bathroom," I said, steering the conversation away from knotting. I set the suitcases down and gestured for her to follow me.

The en-suite had the same open feel with clean lines and dark tile contrasting the white walls. A double vanity took up most of the back wall, with a shower and soaking tub on one side and a steam room on the other.

"You have a sauna. In your house."

I shrugged. "It's actually a steam room, and it's nice after you come in from the cold."

"Can we get in?" she asked, peering through the glass.

I swiped my tongue over my lips and smirked. I was more than happy to see her naked and sweaty, and it would probably help with the aches and pains she was feeling from the plane ride.

"Alright," I said and undid my belt, pushing my pants down over my legs.

"Well, that was easier than I thought it would be," Pam said with a laugh.

I tapped a few buttons to start the steam room, setting it

to a temperature that wouldn't be stifling because, with the two of us in there, I was certain it would get hot enough.

She tugged her sweater over her head and peeled off her leggings while I fumbled with the buttons on my shirt. Her bra dropped to the floor and I slid down my underwear.

We were naked.

In my house.

Together.

Pam leaned against the bathroom counter, removing her glasses and releasing her hair from the clip holding it up. She fluffed the strands, letting them fall down her shoulders, and pushed out her chest.

Gods, those tits.

Her rosy pink nipples just begging me to touch them.

I sauntered over to her, settling myself between her legs. Gripping her thighs, I hoisted her onto the counter, making her squeak.

"Alistair—" she started.

"Shhh," I mumbled against her neck.

The tips of my fingers grazed over her pert nipples with gentle strokes. I slid lower, placing kisses down her chest until I sucked one of the rosy buds into my mouth.

"Fuck," she moaned, grabbing tight handfuls of my curls and tugging me against her breast.

I gave her nipple a little tug with my teeth, making her gasp.

So sensitive.

With her nipple still in my mouth, I forced her legs wider, trailing my fingers along the pebbled skin of her inner thigh and stopping at her center.

"Do you want me to keep going, sweetheart?" I asked, noticing she wasn't as wet as she'd been earlier in the day. I knew from experience that saliva wasn't the best lubricant and I didn't want to hurt her.

"Do you have any lube?" she asked quietly, like it was something to be embarrassed about.

"Of course I do. It's in the bedroom. I also have something else in there I wanted to show you—but then you said you wanted to get in the steam room."

That piqued her interest because she blurted, "What is it?"

"Why don't you let me show you." I stood and grabbed her legs, holding her against me so I could carry her to the bed. "Wrap your arms around my neck."

"Alistair," she screeched. "You can't carry me."

I grinned, losing myself in those beautiful green eyes. "I can absolutely carry you, babe. I'm a big, strong bull. Now wrap your arms around my neck."

She sighed but complied, wrapping her arms around my neck and holding tight.

My hoofs clicked along the tile, and I carried her over to the bed.

Carefully, I set her down in the center, marveling that a woman this beautiful was my girlfriend, that she was *here* in my bed.

The steam room beeped, drawing me out of my stupor.

"It can wait," she said, breathy and low. "We have all week to use it, and I need you right now."

Well, fuck.

I went over to my nightstand, pulling out a bottle of water-based lube and setting it on top. For a second, I hesitated about showing Pam the toy I'd bought for us.

Would she like it?

I'd scoured the internet for this thing and if I knew her like I thought I did, she would be into it.

I removed the bag from the drawer and offered it to Pam. "Go on. Open it."

She stared at it and then at me before finally opening it.

"Oh. My. Gods," she said, holding the bright green, silicone cock sleeve in her hands. She ran her fingertips over the three ridges lining the top, her eyes wide with excitement. "This reminds me of the lizard aliens!"

"Yep," I said proudly. "I wanted to try something out that was like our books." *Our books.* "The ridge at the base vibrates. I, uh, I hope you don't think it's weird."

She shook her head. "Of course I don't think it's weird. It's thoughtful, and I mean, you reading the book was thoughtful, even."

"Books. I've read up to book four."

What could I say?

They were addicting.

"You're something else, Alistair Reid."

She was everything. The happiness I never thought I'd find.

"Do you want to try it?" I asked.

Her eyes widened and she nodded her head.

"Why don't you get yourself ready for me? Play with that pussy so I can get nice and hard."

Pam held out her hand and I drizzled lube onto her fingertips. To get a better view, I walked to the foot of the bed, watching as she ran her slick fingers up and down the seam of her cunt.

"Just like that, babe. Get that pussy glistening for my cock." I pumped my sheath a few times until the curved length of my shaft emerged from the tip.

Lubing up my cock and the alien sleeve, I slid it onto my shaft with some difficulty, stopping right where my own sheath started.

I'd bought the largest size available, but it was still a snug fit.

"What do you think?" I asked, grabbing my cock and running my thumb over the sleeve.

"Hot," she said with a heavy breath, her fingers tracing tiny circles over her clit.

I crawled up the bed and positioned myself between her legs. "Ready?"

"Yeah." She brushed her bangs out of her eyes and nodded.

Pushing the tiny button on the sleeve, it started with a hum, sending waves of vibrations down my shaft that made me shudder.

Maybe this was for me as much as it was for her.

I ran the tip of my cock along her pussy a few times, then slowly pushed it inside.

Pam let out a breathy whine, her hips thrusting forward like she was desperate to take me deeper.

"Easy, sweetheart. Nice and slow," I whispered against her temple, easing the first ridge inside and feeling her cunt stretch around me.

She was so tight, and even with lube, there was no way I was just going to ram this thing inside of her.

"Fuck, I missed you," she groaned.

"I missed you, too." I looked down between us, to where the vibrating ridge was about to make contact with her clit. "And I'm about to make you feel so good."

I thrust hard until the ridge teased her clit, and my cock was as deep as it could go.

"Fuck," she gasped.

"Do you like that, sweetheart?" I asked, drawing out and sliding back in again.

"Yes." She tipped her head back, her red hair matching the color of her flushed cheeks. "This thing is amazing."

"You're amazing. I've thought about this cunt every day since we've been apart. You have no idea how bad I've wanted to fill you with my cum, then fall asleep holding you."

"Kiss me." It wasn't her asking; it was her telling me, letting me know she needed me just as much as I needed her.

My lips crashed into hers for a wild kiss, our teeth clattering, and the two of us panting into one another's mouths while our tongues tangled. I fucked her with feral snaps of my hips, the vibrating outer ridge of the sleeve massaging her clit with each one—but somehow, it didn't feel like it was enough.

"How about we test that flexibility, hmm?" I said between kisses. "Let me stretch you out after that long plane ride."

"You can do whatever you want to me, but gods, please don't stop."

I chuckled, pulling out of her just enough to slide my arms behind her knees. Slowly, I pushed her legs forward and leaned into her, angling the ridge right onto her clit.

"Is this okay?" I asked, not wanting to hurt her.

She shuddered beneath me, her cunt already clenching my cock. "Mhmm."

"Good." I started to move before the word left my lips, driving myself into her so hard that my balls clapped against her ass with each thrust.

"Alistair," she whined, arching her back, pushing those gorgeous tits out and pinching her nipples between her fingertips.

Her cunt clenched me tight, and she moaned, her body

spasming beneath me from her orgasm. I fucked her through it until I came with a loud groan and filled her pussy with my cum.

"Damn," I huffed, and turned off the vibrator. Carefully lowering her legs, I leaned forward and caged her in with my arms.

"Damn is right."

With my cock holding back the floodgates, I laughed and stared down at her. Both of our chests were heaving, the two of us damp with sweat.

"You are so beautiful, Pam Rollins. I'm positive I'm the luckiest minotaur in the world." Hoisting myself up on one arm, I ran my thumb along her jawline until she gave me a contented smile.

"How are you always so romantic?" she asked, running her hands through my chest hair—my very sweaty chest hair.

"Well, I guess I've always been thoughtful—but when it's someone you truly care about, their happiness becomes your happiness. That's when it becomes romantic, and that's how I feel about you." I answered her as best as I could, knowing that I hadn't been like this with other women, not even Chai's mother.

It was very telling.

"I, uh, I'm gonna pull out now." *Real romantic, Alistair. Way to ruin the moment.*

She worried her lip. "We forgot to put a towel down again."

I laughed and shook my head. "I have more duvets."

I looked down between us and slowly pulled out, watching the stream of cum flow out of her cunt and resisting the urge to force it back in like I'd done last time.

"You like watching it, don't you?" she asked, glancing down her naked body at me.

"I do. There's something primal about marking you like that."

It was a shame I didn't know her when I was in my prime. I would have filled her with my cum, breeding her over and over again.

"I like it too."

I grinned and got off the bed. "Let me grab a towel."

I was more than happy to clean up the mess I'd made of her.

I slid off the sleeve, dropped it in the bathroom sink, and grabbed a towel for Pam. I'd thought about coercing her into the shower, but it was late, and she looked exhausted.

When I walked back into the bedroom, I stopped to admire how she looked sprawled out on my bed. I still couldn't believe that this was real.

That she was here.

I joined her on the bed and gently ran the towel between her legs until I'd wiped away most of the cum.

"All done," I said, and pressed a little kiss to her knee.

She propped herself up on her elbows. "Such a gentleman."

I threw the towel in the hamper and slipped on a pair of sweats that sat low on my waist.

"Damn," Pam said with a sigh. "Those are hot."

"It's sweatpants season, babe." I put my arms behind my head, posing against the wall like a Calvin Klein model and swishing my tail all slow and sensual, making her snort.

She grabbed some clothes from her suitcase and slipped into the bathroom, closing the door behind her.

I pulled the duvet off the bed, and on my way back from the linen closet, I found Remi climbing up the stairs.

"Hey buddy," I said, calling him over to me with a pss, pss, pss.

He meowed and rubbed against my legs, obviously happy to see me.

"Come on. Let's go get your mama."

Dutifully, he followed me down the hall into the bedroom.

"I found Remi," I told Pam from behind the door. "He seems to have made himself at home."

She stepped out of the bathroom wearing a tattered Alanis Morisette t-shirt and pink flannel shorts.

I made a mental note to see if Alanis was still touring because if so, I was definitely surprising Pam's little '90s alternative-loving heart with tickets.

Remi bolted over to her, rubbing against her body and purring loud enough that I could hear it from clear across the room.

"He is so freaking cute," I said, sneaking a glance at the two of them while I spread the fresh duvet over the bed.

"He's cute right now, but we'll see how you feel about him in the morning." She yawned and walked over to the bed with Remi on her heels. "This side?" She pointed to the side *without* the omegaverse book on the nightstand.

"Yep. All yours, sweetheart."

For as long as she wanted it.

She climbed under the covers and Remi jumped up to join her.

I shut off the lights, shrouding the room in total darkness. "Is this alright?"

"It's perfect."

I got in bed and she snuggled against me, burying her face in my chest hair.

"I lied," she murmured. "Now it's perfect."

NINETEEN

PAM

I wake up every morning excited for the day ahead.

"Remi," I huffed. "We're on vacation. Can't you give Mama a break?" Completely unfazed, he settled in the dip in my hip and started to make biscuits.

I was so cozy, nestled under the covers and up against Alistair's warm body. His bed smelled like him, that woodsy sage and cedar scent, and I was in no rush to leave it.

But my duties as a cat mom called.

Alistair turned toward me, his curls a wild mess from sleep but still looking as handsome as ever.

Gods, it was nice to wake up to him like this. I couldn't believe this was real, that I was really here.

Remi crept off of me and over to Alistair out of desperation.

"He's a persistent little thing," he said, his voice gravelly from sleep.

I groaned again. "You're telling me. Twice a day, every day. I'm the food bitch."

"Well, while you're here, I'm more than happy to be the food bitch if you tell me what I need to do. The two of you are my guests."

I could never get Don to help make our kids breakfast and get them ready for school, but here was Alistair offering to take care of my cat.

He made an amazing partner.

"Why don't I feed him breakfast, and you can do dinner? I might as well get up and do my morning yoga while I'm at it."

He wrapped his arm around my waist and pulled me against his body. "You don't want me to make you some breakfast first?"

I ran my hands through his curls, admiring how his long lashes fanned out over his chestnut eyes. "I like to get my morning practice in before I eat. But you're more than welcome to have breakfast waiting for me when I'm done."

He gave me one of his signature lopsided smiles. "It would be my pleasure. Why don't you set up in the living room? You can look out over the valley while you practice yoga, and I can watch you from the kitchen."

"You want to watch me?" I asked in shock.

He nodded, his horn rustling back and forth over the pillow. "Of course I do. You. In tight spandex. Moving your body in all sorts of ways. Why wouldn't I want to watch that?"

He had a point there.

I wouldn't mind seeing him in spandex, either.

"Alright. Since you're making me breakfast, I guess you can watch."

I kissed his pink, velvety nose, but when I tried to get up, he pulled me tighter.

"Pam." He caressed my cheek with his thumb, and my heart fluttered. "I'm really happy you're here."

"I'm happy I'm here, too." All of it was worth it. The distance, the flight, everything. Sharing these moments with Alistair, in person, was worth it all.

Remi jumped on my shoulder, digging his nails in to maintain his balance.

"Alright, alright!" I hissed and shooed him off. "I'm coming."

Alistair finally released me from his grip, and I reluctantly climbed out of bed. The moment my feet hit the floor, a shiver rattled through me.

Shit, he kept this place cold, but then again, I wasn't covered in hair.

Remi sat on Alistair's chest, getting pets and waiting patiently while I rifled through my suitcase.

I'd packed quite a few sets of matching tank tops and leggings for the trip, but ultimately decided on an olive green set—one that matched my favorite scarf and my eyes.

Alistair rose up on his elbows and whistled. "I'm not sure I'll be able to focus on cooking breakfast with you looking like that. I might get distracted and burn the pancakes."

I slid my glasses onto my face, laughing. "Someone is flirtatious this morning."

"You're just so beautiful I can't help myself."

"Thank you." My cheeks heated, and I bent over to grab my yoga supplies and the sequence Chai had written for me. "I'm going to head down and get Remi fed."

Alistair stretched with a deep yawn before rolling out of

bed. He walked over to me slowly, his sweatpants sitting just below his belly and his hairy chest displayed in all its glory.

"I'll be down in a few. Let me know if you need help with anything, okay?"

I nodded, and he ran his hand over the column of my neck, wrapping it around the nape and pulling me in for a kiss.

Suddenly the prospect of an early morning yoga session was less appealing.

He pulled away, flashing me a little wink before he strolled into the bathroom and shut the door behind him.

What a tease!

I puffed out a breath, fighting to calm my libido on the walk down to the main floor. Remi raced down the stairs in front of me like he'd lived here his entire life. Calm and confident. Or maybe he was just hungry.

Once I'd given him some wet food and kibbles, I marched down the hall toward the living room.

The living room.

If you could even call it that.

Everything was so open, and the windows allowed the early morning light to pour into the space.

I loved my home in Briar Glenn, but I wouldn't mind living in a place like this.

I spread my mat over the hardwood floors and took a moment to stretch, reviewing Chai's notes. It was so incredibly kind of her to write out the sequences from the classes I was missing while I was here. When I told her I'd be missing class because I was visiting her father, her face lit up. I was glad there wasn't any awkwardness between the two of us.

After starting the meditative playlist on my phone, I

threw my hair up and stepped to the center of my mat. For a few minutes, I sat there, listening to the droning of the music, readying myself for my practice, thankful that my body allowed me to move so freely.

"Mind if I join you?"

I opened my eyes to find Alistair spreading out a yoga mat beside me.

"Really?" I asked in shock.

He grinned and sat cross-legged on his mat with a groan. "Really. I told you I wanted to take up yoga this year. The fact that it's one of your hobbies happens to be an added bonus. I'll warn you, though, I've just been following these online videos that Chai recommended. I haven't taken any classes—yet."

"Why didn't you tell me?"

"I wanted to surprise you."

Tears welled up in my eyes because I was awed again by how thoughtful he was. Alistair was everything I'd spent the last few years reading about, all the things I wanted but thought I'd never have.

He was all the things I deserved.

I was finally in a place where I could admit that.

"Hey," he said, reaching over and caressing my thigh. "We can't do yoga if you're crying."

I took off my glasses and wiped away the tears. "It's really sweet, that's all."

"Sweetheart, if you told me you were taking up snake charming, I'd try it. If it interests you, it interests me."

I snorted. "Well, lucky for you, there's only one type of snake I'm interested in charming."

His eyes widened, then he blinked a few times. "Pam Rollins, are you talking about my cock?"

"Maybe," I said with a little shrug of my shoulders.

Alistair threw back his head, his rumbling laugh echoing through the living room. He was so funny, and I felt a little spark of pride each time I made him laugh.

"You can charm my snake anytime," he said when he finally caught his breath.

Little did he know, I fully intended to. I was only here for a week, and I was going to make the most of it.

"Alright. Yoga time." I pulled my legs under me so that I was sitting on my knees. "I'll call out the moves and you follow along as best as you can, okay?"

With some difficulty, he mimicked my position. "You got it, boss."

I smiled and shook my head. This was going to be interesting.

"PHEW." Alistair puffed out a breath. "That was a workout."

"You did great!" I didn't have the heart to tell him I'd taken it easy and slowed things down because of the altitude.

"This summer, we'll have to do a class at Red Rocks. Chai's done it a few times when she was here visiting."

"She mentioned that when I said I was flying out to see you. I saw some pictures online, and it looks amazing."

"It is. I've been to a few concerts there."

"Speaking of amazing views." I rose from my mat, walked over to the window, and was met with a sight that took my breath away.

Resisting the urge to touch the glass, I got as close as I could without smudging it. The sun was cresting over the valley, the warm light reflecting off the snowy mountain tops and shining on the town below.

"It's beautiful," I whispered under my breath.

There was movement behind me, then Alistair's warm hands gripped my waist. I was so distracted by the view that I didn't hear him get up.

He trailed his nose along my neck, his nose-ring cool against my sweaty skin. "Not nearly as beautiful as this view."

I laughed and reached back, running my fingers through his hair. "No way."

"Yes way," he mumbled, kissing his way down my neck and grinding his cock against my back.

"Alistair." My voice was breathy and I felt flushed—and not just from yoga.

He slipped his hands into the waistband of my leggings and cupped my pussy, making me gasp. "Let me show you just how beautiful I think you are."

I nodded, and he moved quickly, pulling my top up and pressing me against the window. He was frantic, desperate to have me then and there.

Even though I was sweaty from yoga, unshowered from the plane ride and sex the night before, it was the sexiest I'd ever felt.

The glass fogged from my breath, and I shuddered from the cold. I wished I could see what I looked like from the other side with my tits pressed against the glass.

He dropped to his knees and rolled my leggings down, tossing them off to the side.

"Spread those legs for me, sweetheart," he groaned, his fingers sliding up the back of my thighs.

I widened my stance and pushed my ass out, inviting him to taste me. He forced himself between my legs, the length of his snout and his tongue giving him access to my pussy.

The first swipe of the textured pad of his tongue along my center made me moan.

"Gods, you taste so fucking good." His voice was muffled, but I could feel every word as they left his lips.

How did I go without this for so many years?

It didn't really matter because now I had a partner who didn't just like to eat; he liked to feast.

Alistair pulsed his tongue in and out, making me pant. He wrapped one of his hands around the front of my thigh. With the tips of his fingers, he rubbed gentle circles over my clit, continuing to fuck me with his tongue.

"Alistair," I whined, feeling my orgasm build and making him groan.

"Come for me, beautiful. Come on my mouth," he rasped before forcing his tongue inside my pussy again.

The cold on my nipples, the warmth of his tongue, his fingers on my clit. All the sensations hit me at once and my orgasm tore through me.

"Oh, gods!" I screamed against the glass.

Alistair supported my quivering body, his grip the only thing keeping me from sliding down the glass and dropping to the floor.

He swirled lazy circles over my clit until my orgasm subsided and my body stilled.

"I've got you. I've got you," he whispered, carefully pulling me onto the floor with him.

"Shit." I sat between his legs, leaning against his chest while I caught my breath. "An orgasm like that, and I haven't even eaten breakfast yet. What a way to start the day."

He wrapped his arms around me and kissed the top of my head. "I already ate my breakfast."

I shook my head, and he chuckled.

"Pushing me up against the window was a nice touch," I said, looking up at him.

He grinned. "You liked that?"

I nodded. "We have to clean the glass now, though."

"Says who? Maybe I like your tit prints on the glass. Every time I see it, I'll think of you and how much I like making you come."

"Would you like me to return the favor?" Even though I was completely spent, I could feel the press of his dick against me.

"Nah," he said with a shake of his head. "We have all week for that. And don't ever feel like you need to reciprocate. I like making you feel good. It isn't like it's some chore. It's for me just as much as it's for you."

It was something I'd never felt with Don. Sex had always been about him and his pleasure. Not once in all our years of marriage did he ever care about getting me off—and Alistair was out here giving me orgasms like it was an Olympic sport and he was after a gold medal.

And, *spoiler alert*, he'd win a gold medal and more.

"Alright, let me get started on breakfast." He rose with a groan, helping me to my feet. " Are pancakes and fruit okay?"

I pulled my tank down over my boobs and grabbed my underwear and leggings from where he'd tossed them. "That sounds good to me," I said, shimmying my leggings over my thighs.

Alistair strolled into the kitchen, his tail calmly swishing behind him and his sweats clinging to his ass.

I snorted, remembering last night when he'd leaned up

against the wall like he was some kind of model. Honestly, he could have been one, even now. The silver fox, daddy vibe was in.

"What's so funny?" he asked as he set to work on the pancake batter.

"I was just thinking about how you give off daddy vibes."

"Oh, like those mountain man books?"

"Yes, like those." He really did absorb everything I told him.

He grimaced. "I just can't do the whole daddy thing. Not to yuck anyone's yum, but there's only one person in my life that calls me that."

"How do you know about 'yucking someone's yum'?"

He refused to look at me, focusing on the pancake batter like it held life's secrets instead. "I joined some spicy book reader groups..."

"Alistair!"

"What?" He grinned, and I would have bet money he was blushing underneath his hair. "I've learned a lot from them. That's how I found the sex club book."

Gods, he was everything.

"Anyway..." He dropped a scoop of batter onto the pan. "What's on the agenda for today? Breakfast, shower, any other requests?"

"I flew out here to see you and give you some support while you work through things. We don't need to get all crazy and do a bunch of sightseeing. You know I'm a homebody."

With perfect knife skills, he cut up a strawberry and handed me a slice.

"I was thinking I'd show you around the house and property today, then tonight we can go into Denver for dinner. It's supposed to snow all day tomorrow, so I figured we could bum around the house. But we do have plans for Valentine's Day."

"You didn't have to do all that..." I mumbled through a mouthful of strawberry.

"Of course I did. You flew all the way out here. And if anyone deserves romance, it's you."

TWENTY

ALISTAIR

"Nothing is worth more than this day. You cannot relive yesterday. Tomorrow is still beyond your reach." —Johann Wolfgang von Goethe

---

I still couldn't get over the fact that Pam was here.

Last night we had a romantic dinner at the best Italian restaurant in Denver. The combination of carbs, copious amounts of wine, and the heavy snowfall meant that we'd spent most of today snuggled up in bed, eating junk food and watching old movies.

I had zero complaints.

"We should probably eat some real food," I said and ran my finger over Pam's shoulder. It was dotted with these adorable little freckles, likely from being out in the sun, but I thought they were one of the prettiest things about her.

She snuggled closer, burying her face in my chest hair. "But I'm so warm, and you smell so good."

"Why don't I give you one of my sweatshirts to wear. I

know that's like the ultimate sign of affection, and I prob-ably won't get it back."

She braced herself up on her elbow and stared me down. "I mean, I did give you my favorite scarf."

"An eye for an eye, I suppose," I said with a grin. "Come on."

She followed me into the walk-in closet, and I pointed to where my hoodies hung clustered together.

"Take your pick."

"Hmm," she said, her fingers trailing across the sleeves.

Gods, I hope she doesn't pick my favorite…

It was like she could read my thoughts.

She stopped at my well-loved Rutherford University hoodie—the one with a half zip to accommodate my horns. Bringing the sleeve up to her nose, she inhaled deeply.

"This one."

Of. Fucking. Course.

But if I was going to give my hoodie to anyone, it would be her.

"That one's my favorite," I said, and her expression dropped.

"I can pick another—"

I stepped closer, taking the hoodie off of the hanger and handing it to her with a sincere smile. "No, I want you to have it. Every time you wear it, you'll think of me. The same way I think of you when I wear your scarf."

She smiled and scraped her teeth over that full lower lip of hers. "Thank you."

Without warning, she lifted her tattered Alanis shirt over her head, giving me a glimpse of her tits.

Gods, I wish I could have been on the other side of that glass yesterday.

She pulled the hoodie over her head before I could act

on all the devious thoughts racing through my mind, her significantly smaller body practically drowning in it.

"How do I look?" She pulled up the zipper and gave me a little twirl with her arms flapping in the sleeves.

"Adorable." I was utterly enamored with this woman. She was all the trouble I'd anticipated and more.

She grabbed her glasses from the nightstand and followed me down to the living room, then over to the windows.

"It's really coming down out there. Obviously, we get snow in Briar Glenn, but it's nothing like this."

I tsked, watching the fat snowflakes cover the deck. "The roads are probably a mess."

She leaned against me. "Perfect for a night in."

A perfect night for something else...

"Would you, uh, would you want to take an edible?" I asked shyly.

I didn't want her to feel pressured, but it was something I enjoyed.

"Alright," she said with a shrug. "When in Rome."

I chuckled and shook my head. "It's still crazy to me that someone with a deep love for '90s alternative has never smoked pot."

"Alistair, I lived in small town U.S.A., watching Nirvana unplugged while my kids were down for their nap. It wasn't exactly like I had a ton of opportunities. Besides, Don would have flipped his lid."

Don.

I hated that motherfucker.

Or maybe I was just jealous that he got to spend so many years with her while I was left soaking up whatever time with her I could.

"Well, today that changes. This way to the stash drawer, madame."

"You have an entire drawer?" She asked and followed me into the kitchen.

"Yes, I have a drawer. I'm CEO of a cannabis company, remember?" I pulled the drawer open, and the skunky scent of pot wafted out.

"Goodness." She wrinkled her nose. "That is pungent."

"I take it you've never been to a concert either?"

She shook her head.

Yeah. I was taking her to see Alanis.

"You know, I want you to make a list of all the things you've always wanted to do but never got the chance to, and we're going to work our way down the list. We can check off 'plane ride' and 'edibles.'"

Anything she wanted, I'd foot the bill. We'd do it all.

"Don't you think you've done enough for me?"

I grabbed her hip, tugging her to me for a quick kiss. "Sweetheart, this is just the beginning. Now, let's see."

I flipped through the pouches and packets, searching for something that wouldn't have her cemented to the couch for four hours. I should have prepared for this ahead of time, but I wasn't sure she'd say yes.

Two and a half milligrams was probably good for her first time.

Right?

It had been a long time since I took a low dose like that, but with edibles, things could go bad fairly quickly.

I could only imagine that phone call.

"Hey Tegan, I overdosed your mom with edibles. She saw the goddess and panicked. We're at the emergency room, but she's going to be fine!"

I stopped on a packet of pink lemonade gummies that were exactly two and a half milligrams.

Those would work.

I grabbed a gummy out of the packet and held it out to her. "These are a really low dosage. They're what Chai normally takes. It'll take about thirty minutes to kick in and be more of a body high. You'll probably want to just chill on the couch."

She went to grab the gummy but hesitated. "Are you sure you don't need my help with dinner? I don't want to get all stoned and be a burden."

"You're never a burden. I like cooking for you." I lowered my voice and whispered, "Plus, you make me nervous when you use a knife."

She snorted and snatched the gummy. "Whatever, Mr. Top Chef," she grumbled.

"Make sure you chew it up. Don't just swallow it."

She chewed dramatically, making me laugh. I loved seeing her like this—goofy and playful—because I got the impression she was never like this with Don.

I popped my own gummy, and while I chewed, I got us a glass of water to share.

Pam took a long drink, then passed me the glass. "Those taste awful. What are they supposed to be?" She picked up the package and read the label. "Pink lemonade? Maybe pink lemonade mixed with dirt."

"Yeah, I should have warned you. No matter what you do, that marijuana 'taste' is still there."

"Your company should work on that."

I'd been dodging any efforts she made to talk about the company or Jonathan's offer. I was having such a great time with her; I didn't want to think about it.

Time to change the subject.

"Do you want to listen to some music?" I asked, walking over to the shelf that held my record collection.

She followed behind me, her eyes scanning the titles. "This is quite the collection. You'd get along with Reece's mate, Cyrus. He's a big record collector."

"I'd really like to meet them. Your kids and their mates." I knew they were the most important people in the world to her. I'd heard so many stories that I felt like I knew them already.

"I'd really like that." She slid a record off the shelf and handed it to me.

Tom Petty and the Heartbreakers Greatest Hits.

"A classic. Great choice, babe."

"I thought Tom Petty was appropriate for my first marijuana experience."

"It really is. Why don't you go make yourself comfortable?" I slid the record out of the sleeve, and by the time the intro to "American Girl" started, Pam was already snuggled under a blanket with Remi in her lap.

"You two are cute." I sat beside them, wrapping my arm around Pam's shoulder and pulling her closer.

"No, you are." She sang the chorus under her breath. "I love this song."

"I mean, you lived it."

"Pretty much." She grabbed my hand, her thumb rubbing over my fingers. "But now I know there's more to life. So much more."

I grinned and kissed her forehead because I felt the exact same way.

We sat like that for a while, cuddled together and vibing to the music until the first side of the record was over.

"How are you feeling?" I asked.

She looked at me and smiled. Her eyes were glassy, the

green made more vibrant by the red surrounding them. "I feel good."

"You look like you feel good," I said with a smirk, even though I was sure I looked the same way. "Are you hungry?"

She nodded.

"I'll make us something to eat."

Her face lit up. "That would be amazing. Can you flip the record too?"

"Already planned on it, sweetheart."

I gave her a throw pillow to use in my place and pushed myself off of the couch with a groan.

Yesterday's yoga routine had proven to be quite the workout.

I flipped the record and went to the kitchen, sneaking a glance at Pam on the couch. She was slumped against the pillow with her eyes closed, petting Remi, and mouthing the words to "Don't Do Me Like That."

She was definitely feeling it. I was just glad she was *enjoying* it.

"Hey, American Girl. What are you in the mood for?" I called out to her over the music.

Her eyes fluttered open and she thought for a second. "Can you make me a grilled cheese?"

While that wasn't exactly what I had in mind when I told her we needed to eat some real food, who was I to deny her? It was her first time having the munchies, after all.

"You got it, pretty lady. One grilled cheese, coming right up."

I grabbed the butter and cheese from the fridge, and when I turned around, Pam was sitting at the island.

"You didn't have to get up, babe. I would have brought it over to you."

She shook her head. "I wanted to keep you company."

"Well, thank you. Thirsty?" I asked, noticing how scratchy her voice sounded.

She nodded, and when I passed her the water, she drained the glass.

"Gods, you're wonderful," she said, wiping her mouth with the sleeve of *my* hoodie.

"Wonderful? You can call me Al."

She snorted. "I was so worried you were going to think that joke was stupid."

I flipped her grilled cheese then leaned over the counter to look at her. "It wasn't stupid at all. That's how I knew we were going to hit it off. And we've been hitting it off every day since."

I thought about her all day, every day. Wondering what she was doing and when I'd get to talk to her next. Wishing I could see her.

And here she was.

We'd seamlessly slipped into a routine like we'd never been apart. Like this was natural. Like together was where we belonged.

I plated her sandwich and slid it in front of her. "Dinner is served."

She picked it up immediately, digging right into it with a big bite.

I raised my brows in anticipation, and she gave me a thumbs-up.

"This is so freaking good," she mumbled through a mouthful of food.

"I'm glad. Only the best for you."

"Are you going to make one for yourself?"

I shook my head and headed to the pantry, grabbing a bulk-size jar of peanut butter and setting it on the counter.

"You aren't allergic, are you?" I asked, remembering that it was a pretty common allergen.

Again, the last thing we needed was an ER visit.

"Nope."

I slathered a slice of bread with a generous serving of peanut butter and slapped another piece of bread on top.

"You aren't going to put any jelly on that?" Pam asked, her mouth hanging open when I looked her dead in the eye and took a big bite.

"Nope." My speech was garbled from the sandwich sticking to the roof of my already dry mouth.

Her eyes narrowed. "I was convinced you weren't a serial killer, but now I'm not so sure."

"This was all part of my plan. Coerce you out here, give you orgasms, and make you eat peanut butter sandwiches sans jelly."

She snorted and brought her hand up to her mouth. "The orgasms are worth it."

"They're about all I'm good for."

"You're good for all the things."

Just as I shoved the last bite of the sandwich into my mouth, "Here Comes My Girl" started to play.

I forced my food down and walked over to Pam.

"Dance with me." I extended my hand out to her, demanding rather than asking.

She briefly looked at my outstretched palm, then slid her dainty little hand into mine.

I slipped my other hand around her waist, leaning over slightly to make up for our size difference, and slowly led her around the kitchen.

Tom Petty's voice rasped, flowed soft and smooth, then rasped again. I locked eyes with Pam, grinning like a fool because the lyrics conveyed all the things I felt about her.

It was snowing. We were stoned out of our minds, and she was all I needed tonight. I spun her just as the music faded before bringing her close and dipping her with a soft kiss.

She gazed up at me as I pulled away, her chest heaving. "You're a good dancer."

I chuckled. "Much better than I am at ice skating?"

"Definitely better than you are at ice skating."

I grinned and ran my thumb along her jaw. "What do you wanna do now, sweetheart?"

She looked over at the couch where Remi was snuggled up on a blanket. "Maybe we can watch the snow?"

"I'd love that. Why don't you go wait for me on the couch?"

"Okay," she said on the tail end of a yawn. It reminded me of that first night we talked on the phone—when we were both nervous about our date.

Here we were a month and a half later, and I couldn't imagine my life without her.

I stopped the record player and dimmed the lights before joining her on the couch.

"Lay your head in my lap. Stretch out and get comfortable."

"Are you sure? Isn't that going to be uncomfortable for you?"

"I'll be fine. Give me your glasses, and I'll set them on the armrest." I knew she was going to fall asleep, but if this was what she wanted, I'd happily give it to her.

She put the pillow on my lap, handed me her glasses, and laid her head down, wriggling closer until she was comfortable. Her red hair cascaded down her back, practically begging me to touch it.

Giving into temptation, I stroked my fingers over the crown of her head, making her hum.

"That feels nice," she said, her voice heavy.

"Good."

Remi snuggled up beside her, and I could barely make out her fingers slowly stroking his back.

Fluffy white snowflakes continued to fall, blanketing the mountains with a fresh layer of snow.

It was perfect for what I had planned for tomorrow.

Eventually, Pam's breathing slowed and her hand stilled. Remi wriggled out from under her palm, carefully stepped over her head, and climbed onto my chest.

He was such a cool cat.

"Remi," I whispered. "When you go back home, remind your mama how special she is. How she lights up a room with her smile and that her snort is the prettiest thing I've ever heard."

I scratched his chin, and he said he would—well, not with his words—but that's how I interpreted his contented purr.

Leaning back, I closed my eyes and smiled to myself because *this...*

It was everything my life had been missing.

TWENTY-ONE

PAM

I am worthy of good things.

"Happy Valentine's Day, sweetheart."

My eyes fluttered open at the sound of that familiar, gruff voice.

I blinked a few times, my vision clearing to show Alistair standing beside the bed with a tray in his hands.

"What's all this?" I asked, reaching for my glasses on the nightstand.

"Breakfast in bed. I wanted to surprise you."

I propped myself up on the pillows, and Al passed me the tray. He'd cooked me a full spread: fluffy scrambled eggs, waffles, and bacon. A vase of bright wildflowers sat in the corner with a card propped up against them.

Regardless of whatever else Alistair had planned for today, this already beat past Valentine's Days.

I felt like the luckiest woman in the world.

Looking up at Al, I could feel my lip quivering. As

usual, he was so ridiculously thoughtful. "Thank you," I said, my voice wavering.

"Why don't you open the card?" He raised his brows, that lopsided grin curving up one corner of his mouth.

I grabbed the bright pink envelope and flipped it open.

On the front of the card, there was a cellphone that read 'we took a chance on what could be' with 'thank you for swiping right on me' on the inside, followed by a hand-written note:

Happy Valentine's Day

I appreciate you coming all this way to see me. It means more to me than you could ever know.

XOXO

Al

A folded piece of paper was tucked inside, a print out of a one year membership at the hot yoga studio in Rock Harbor. That was an affluent area, so I was positive the membership wasn't cheap.

I clutched the card to my chest. "Thank you so much."

"Anything for you." He leaned over, stroking his thumb over my cheek and placing a soft kiss on top of my head.

"I have something for you, too."

Sweater curse be damned, I couldn't wait to give him what I'd been working on.

"You go ahead and eat first. I don't want your breakfast getting cold."

"Aren't you going to eat?" I asked, already cutting up my eggs.

He sat down at the foot of the bed and shook his head. "I, uh, I tend to pick at the food while I'm cooking."

I snorted, because I did the same thing when I cooked for other people, and took a sip of my coffee.

Shit.

He even made it how I liked it.

"So what do you have planned today, loverboy? Taking me to a ski chalet? A plane ride to Paris? A yacht trip around the world?"

I was only half joking. With Alistair, none of those would be all that surprising.

"Nothing that grand for today, I'm afraid. Did you bring your cold weather gear?"

I nibbled on a slice of bacon and nodded.

"Good. You're going to need it today."

Well, my curiosity was piqued.

Cross-country skiing? Snowshoe hiking?

He stood up with a groan and sauntered over to the closet. "You finish up. I'm gonna get dressed."

By the time he returned, I'd eaten as much as I could and sucked down every last drop of my coffee.

"All done with this?" he asked.

"I'm stuffed. It was delicious."

He was dressed in a white v-neck t-shirt with black snow pants covering his lower half, and when he turned around—I noticed I couldn't see his tail.

"Where's your tail?"

He twisted to look at his butt before grinning at me. "I tucked it into my pants. It gets cold out on the trails."

Fuck, he was adorable.

And it made total sense. His tail wasn't fluffy like Atlas'.

He started for the door and I stopped him before he could turn the corner.

"Wait, your gift."

I threw off the covers and removed a bundle wrapped in maroon wrapping paper from my suitcase. Somehow it made it through the airport unscathed.

Alistair set the tray on the nightstand and took the package from me. He carefully peeled back the paper, grinning wide when he saw what was inside.

"Pam. No way." He held up the chunky knit cardigan I'd made him out of rust-colored yarn. It matched one of mine and Remi's—my favorite one.

"I had to race to finish it in time. Do you know how hard it was not to spoil the surprise the other day?"

He ran his fingers over the cables I'd knit down the front. "It matches yours and Remi's."

"It does." I beamed up at him. "Do you like it?"

"Like it? I love it. Thank you." Before he even got the last word out, he'd slid his arms into the cardigan. "How do I look?" He gripped the lapels and puffed out his chest.

"As handsome as ever."

"Can we take a picture together? The three of us in matching sweaters?" His words were rushed, his excitement one of the cutest things I had ever seen.

"Of course."

He stepped into my space and wrapped his arms around my waist, pulling me against him. "Thank you."

Leaning in, he kissed me soft and sweet, completely unbothered by my morning breath mixed with the aftertaste of coffee. His fingers traveled up to the column of my neck, wrapping around the nape while he deepened the kiss. I felt myself getting wet, the heat starting between my legs and spreading throughout my body.

I was tempted to beg him to cancel whatever plans he had made and confine him to the bedroom instead.

He pulled away with a laugh, and I groaned.

"There's plenty of time for that later, sweetheart." He nuzzled my temple and whispered in my ear, "Do you really think I'd celebrate Valentine's Day without worshiping your pretty little cunt?"

Holy fuck.

Without another word, he grabbed the tray from the nightstand and headed downstairs, leaving me standing there panting.

It was just plain cruel.

I brushed my teeth and dressed as quickly as possible, layering moisture-wicking long-johns under my snow pants and sweater. The snow boots I'd brought felt clunky on my feet as I clopped down the stairs, but at least they'd be warm.

Alistair stood in the living room with Remi cradled in his arms. He'd already dressed the little man in his sweater.

"He didn't give you any trouble, did he?" Remi was used to wearing sweaters, but normally, I was the one that put them on.

Alistair scratched Remi's chin, the cat practically melting under his touch. "He was a perfect angel. Just like he always is. Come stand over here. I have my phone set up."

Alistair's phone was propped against a stack of records pointed at the fireplace. I threw my hair up into a clip and joined the two of them.

Alistair wrapped his free arm around my shoulder, and I rested mine on the small of his back.

"You ready?" he asked.

I fluffed my bangs and adjusted my glasses. "How are you going to take the picture from all the way over here?"

"I have a Bluetooth button. That's how I take selfies on hiking trips."

"Technology."

He chuckled. "Alright, on the count of three. One, two, three."

I stared at the camera and smiled, genuinely smiled, because I was here with him. Wearing matching sweaters and taking pictures with my boyfriend and my cat.

It was every cat lover's dream.

Alistair set Remi down and rushed over to his phone. Sliding his finger across the screen, he said, "Holy shit, these are adorable."

I walked over to him, wrapping my hands around his arm and pulling his phone down so I could see the pictures.

Alistair and I looked adorable, the two of us in our sweaters and snow pants, holding one another and smiling brightly. Remi was gazing up at Alistair with complete and utter adoration. A look he'd only shown one other person: me.

It was perfect.

"Can you send me that?" I asked and my phone vibrated in my pocket.

"Already done, sweetheart. You ready to have some fun?"

"Yep. The suspense is killing me."

We put on our coats and Alistair led me through the garage, around the back of the house, and down to a large storage shed. He had already shoveled a path, so I didn't have to trudge through the deep snow.

He stopped in front of the shed. "Close your eyes, babe."

I did as he asked, enjoying the fact that he was excited and building this up so much.

The rolling door to the shed slid up with a loud clang.

"Open your eyes."

Sitting in the center of the shed was a shiny minotaur-size snowmobile with two helmets hanging from the handlebars.

Alistair stood next to it with his hands on his hips, grinning wide. "Thought you might like to take a little ride through the mountains."

"Uh, yes, please." My body pressed up against Alistair's while we zoomed around the mountainside? I was sold.

He pushed the snowmobile down a ramp into the snow. Taking one of the helmets off the handlebars, he passed it to me. "Put this on. Safety first."

I looked at the slip-on helmet, then up at Alistair. "How is that going to work for you?"

He undid the clasps on the sides of his helmet, pulling it into two separate pieces. "It clasps around my horns like this."

Bringing both pieces up to his head, he clicked them together and secured the clasps with a snap. "See," he mumbled.

It was one of the coolest things I had ever seen. I loved that the world had adapted and modified things for monsters.

Alistair hopped on the snowmobile, and I pulled on my helmet and gloves, then slid behind him.

"It's going to be a little loud, so if you want to talk, we'll have to yell. Hold onto my waist and lean when I lean, okay?"

"Okay." Growing up in a small town, I'd ridden on the back of dirt bikes a time or two, so this wasn't all that new to me.

Alistair started the snowmobile and the engine roared. I

snuggled closer, pressing against him and holding onto his waist tightly.

He cranked the throttle, then we were off. The snowmobile flew over the snow, the trees lining the trail blurring to a fuzzy haze of green and white. Peeking around Alistair's hulking body, I saw the valley and the town off in the distance. I'd always thought Briar Glenn was picturesque, but it was nothing compared to this.

We rode over a series of hills and my stomach dropped each time we hit the bottom. I started laughing—that type of uncontrollable laughter that only comes when there's an element of danger. I knew Alistair wouldn't let anything happen, but it was thrilling all the same.

The trail led to an overlook before splitting in two. Alistair pulled a safe distance from the edge, angling the snowmobile sideways so we could enjoy the view.

He unclipped his helmet and hung it over the handlebar, and I tugged mine off too.

"Check out this view, sweetheart." With each of his breaths, a cloud of white smoke jetted from his nostrils.

"I can't get over how beautiful it is."

As much as I was into him, there was no way I could ask him to leave all this behind. The mountains, his house, his job.

There was just no way.

Alistair stepped in front of me. Leaning over, he pressed his forehead to mine. "I'm glad you like it. Happy Valentine's Day, Pam."

He gripped my chin, tilting my face up so he had access to my lips. Our mouths crashed together, tongues tangling and hands roving over the layers that covered our bodies. Even through our snow pants, I could feel Alistair's cock jutting into me, reminding me of just how good it felt when he fucked me.

Suddenly, I was too hot. Too horny. Desperate for him to take me.

"Let's go back home," I mumbled against his lips.

"No. I can't wait. Bend over the snowmobile, and I'll fuck you right here." He took off his gloves and shoved them in his coat pocket.

"What if someone drives by and sees us?" My heart raced at the idea, making me aware of how much I liked these risky rendezvous. Alistair undid the button of my snow pants and slipped his hand inside. He swirled his fingers along my entrance, making my breath hitch.

"Mmm," he hummed. "Already so wet. I think you'd like it if someone rode by and saw me fucking you. Wouldn't you?"

He pumped a finger inside, smiling at the gasp that slipped past my lips. "Go on, babe. Lean over the snowmobile. Enjoy the view while I pound your tight cunt."

Fuck.

I pulled away, walking around the snowmobile and stretching out over the seat.

Alistair came up behind me, and I heard the whir of his zipper. He tugged my pants down just enough to give him access to my pussy, and I shuddered when the cold air hit my skin.

"Now this, this is a perfect view." He ran his palm over my cheek and gave it a soft swat.

"Gods," I groaned. "Again." I never thought I'd be into spanking, but under Alistair's hand, I was very much into it.

He brought his palm down on the other cheek, a little harder this time, the sting warming away the cold and making me moan.

"I like seeing your ass covered in my marks. I might have to spank you more often. Now spread those legs and arch your back."

I spread my legs as much as my bulky pants would allow and pushed my ass out toward Alistair. The snow crunched under his hooves, and I felt the tip of his cock sliding back and forth over my entrance.

He teased me like that, one light thrust after another, just rubbing the tip over my clit.

"Alistair," I whined, growing frustrated.

I wanted to be fucked, not edged.

He chuckled, digging his fingers into my hips; he forced himself inside with a sharp thrust.

"Shit," I moaned, bracing myself against the snowmobile.

He ground his hips against me with a satisfied hum. "Fuck, I love being buried inside of you."

He withdrew slowly only to snap his hips forward and drive himself deep again.

Puffs of breath and little moans of pleasure left me each time he forced himself inside of me.

Alistair released one of my hips, and I braced myself on the seat, knowing what was coming. His hand clapped down on my ass, and I cried out from the heady mix of pain and pleasure.

He leaned over me slightly and ran his fingertips alongside his cock, coating them with my arousal before massaging my clit. With the new position, his thrusts were more shallow, but he increased the speed, slamming into me hard and fast.

Our gasps and grunts were joined by the roar of snowmobiles off in the distance—meaning we weren't the only ones on the trail.

"You hear that, babe?" Alistair asked. "Better hurry up and come for me, or someone might see us."

Someone might see us.

Someone might see my massive minotaur boyfriend railing me against a snowmobile on the side of a mountain.

The thought made my core tighten and my pussy throb.

"You'd like that, wouldn't you? I can feel you getting tight, my little exhibitionist," Alistair chuckled.

He pushed down on me, arching my back as much as he could and burying himself to the hilt. He pressed his fingertips into my clit, rubbing it back and forth in rapid succession—exactly how I liked it.

"I'm so close," he rasped. "You're going to ride back to the house with my cum dribbling out of your cunt. Scream for me, sweetheart. Let everyone know how good I make you feel."

I lost myself to my orgasm, crying out with a series of moans and looking out at the beautiful snow-covered valley below us through hooded eyes.

It was rough and dirty and romantic.

It was all the things I'd come to expect with Alistair.

It was all the things he'd taught me about myself.

It was perfect.

Leaning over me, he thrust hard, his body jolting while he filled me with his cum and fucked me through my orgasm.

"Pam," he groaned.

Over and over again, his cock spasmed inside of me, leaving cum trailing down my thighs.

The rumble of the snowmobiles was getting louder by the second, pulling me out of my post-orgasm haze.

"Fuck," Alistair whispered against my shoulder, giving it a soft kiss before standing upright.

He pulled out, quickly yanking up my snow pants to catch the deluge of cum spilling out of my pussy.

I knew he came a lot—but this—it was so much that it was almost uncomfortable.

He turned me toward him, giving me a sly smile while he tucked his cock back into his pants.

Four snowmobiles raced down the trail toward the overpass but veered left, taking one of the offshoots.

"That was close." My chest heaved, and I felt like my body was on fire despite the cold.

Alistair ran his tongue over his lip and grinned. "I think you would have liked it. Maybe we should look into one of those sex clubs."

"Alistair!"

I mean, it was a no from me at the moment, but I wouldn't rule it out completely.

And if I did something like that with anyone, it would be with him.

He smiled like he knew that and passed me my helmet. "Let's get you home and showered. Oh, and by the way." He leaned in until his whiskers tickled my ear. "No one has ever made me come like that."

TWENTY-TWO

ALISTAIR

"Often when you think you're at the end of something, you're at the beginning of something else." – Fred Rogers

---

Yesterday was like something out of a dream.

Valentine's Day with the most amazing woman I'd ever met. Bending her over a snowmobile and fucking her.

A great dinner with even better company.

A night filled with more amazing sex.

Hell, this entire visit was a dream come true—and I wasn't ready for it to end.

A set of arms hugged my waist, and Pam peeked around me. "What's on the menu for tonight, chef?"

"Seared king oyster mushroom 'scallops' and roasted asparagus. A nice chardonnay. I know it isn't your preferred boxed wine, but it'll have to do."

"Hey," she said, drawing her brows together. "Leave my boxed wine alone."

I dabbed a spoon in the garlic butter sauce I was braising the mushrooms in and held it out to her. "Give it a taste."

I slipped the spoon into her mouth, watching her full lips close around it.

Fuck.

She managed to make the most mundane things so sexy.

"Shit, that's good," she mumbled when I pulled the spoon away.

I loved cooking for her.

She'd spent so many years of her life preparing meals for everyone else. She deserved it.

I jostled the asparagus in the pan, giving it a little poke with the tongs to make sure it wasn't getting mushy. "Can you grab some plates out of the cabinet?" I used the tongs like a pointer, directing Pam to the cabinet that had all the tableware.

"I think I can manage that." She stood on her tiptoes and, with some effort, grabbed two plates that she sat on the counter beside me.

"Why don't you take a seat? Relax a little bit."

She walked around the island and climbed onto one of the stools. "I'm surprised this place doesn't have a dining room."

I grinned and plated our food. "It did. I ripped it out to make the living room bigger, then had the windows and deck added on. It just didn't make sense to have a room I'd never use."

"There's no way I'd be able to live without mine. I need somewhere to put my kids and their mates when they come over for dinner on Sundays. My kitchen can barely fit two people."

I nodded, fighting back a frown. "I, uh, don't really have that problem, living out here alone."

She was quiet like she didn't know what to say.

I wasn't sure what I wanted her to say.

Did I want her to tell me to sell my shares and move to Briar Glenn?

I poured us both a glass of wine and sat down next to her.

There was a noticeable tension between us, like the illusion of the past few days was finally crumbling into reality. Every second that passed brought us closer to having to say goodbye again.

She cleared her throat and popped a 'scallop' into her mouth, chewing it with a little hum. "This is amazing."

"Thank you." I nibbled on a piece of asparagus, having lost my appetite to the ball of nerves in the pit of my stomach.

Pam set her fork down, bracing her arm against the counter as she stared at me. "Al, we have to talk about this at some point. The whole reason I came out here was to support you through this."

I took a hefty swig of my wine, almost draining the glass. "I know. I've just worked so hard to build that company. I'm not sure I'm ready to give it all up."

"You wouldn't be giving it up, you'd be passing it along to Jonathan."

I tsked and shook my head. "You know, that's the funny thing. Twenty years ago, that was me. I was in Jonathan's shoes, watching as the older guys aged out, took their money, and retired—and now I'm the older guy. It's a bitter pill to swallow."

She laughed and gripped my thigh. "What did you

think? That you were going to work until you died? What kind of life would that be?"

"I don't know what I thought. I just—thought I had more time."

That signature snort of hers made me smile. "I know that feeling well."

The death of her husband, his pension transferring over to her, passing the bakery to Tegan. Pam had been through a lot of major life changes over the last few years.

"How did you cope? You were thrown into a lot of things all at once."

She let out a deep breath. "You know, for years, the bakery was the only thing I had outside of the kids and Don. The one thing that was mine, and I'd worked so fucking hard to make it successful. I always hoped Tegan would take it over, but when that day finally came, it was hard giving it up. I felt like I was letting go of the one thing that defined me. But it wasn't the only thing that defined me.

"Sure, there was an adjustment period, but retiring meant I had more time for all those knitting projects I'd set aside. I could watch all the movies and read all the books I'd missed out on. I could spend time with my kids without thinking about work the entire time—I could live in the moment. And if I wasn't retired, I wouldn't have been able to drop everything and fly out here to see you. You might feel like you're losing a part of yourself by selling your shares, but you're gaining something precious, something that we take for granted. Time."

Time.

It was something I'd come to appreciate in my relationship with her. Regardless of how long we spent together, it never felt like it was enough.

I put my hand on top of hers, gripping it tight and losing myself in her emerald eyes. "Well, when you put it like that, there's a lot of things I'd rather spend my time doing besides working."

"Like me?" she said, batting her lashes.

I threw my head back with a bellowing laugh. "Pamela Rollins, I think my sense of humor is rubbing off on you." Leaning over, I lowered my voice and whispered in her ear, "And I'd spend all my time doing you if I could."

"I mean, I wouldn't be opposed to that." She raised her brows and took a sip of her wine.

This woman.

How was I lucky enough to stumble right into her path?

To convince her to date me—long distance—after one date?

Minotaurs didn't have fated mates, but whatever act of the goddess this was, I was thankful I'd been blessed with Pam in my life.

Bringing her hand up to my lips, I placed a soft kiss on her knuckles. "Come on, pretty lady. Let's eat before the food gets cold."

"WHY DON'T you let me help you?" I asked, watching Pam bustle around the kitchen with a countertop cleaner and a roll of paper towels.

"You did the cooking. Let me clean up." She looked across the living room at the fireplace. "Why don't you light a fire? That would be nice and cozy for our last night together."

Our last night together.

The very thought was enough to make me depressed—and she was still here.

"Whatever you want, sweetheart. Tonight is all about you."

I flipped the switch for the damper and set to work stacking the wood. Using a lighter to ignite a ball of lint and wax I'd made myself, I shoved it in the center with a handful of twigs.

That would do the trick.

In a few minutes, we'd have a roaring fire.

Pam stood at the sink with her back to me, humming absentmindedly while she scrubbed a saucepan.

She was wearing leggings and the hoodie I'd given her, the hem hanging down over the back of her thighs because it was so big on her.

Quietly, I crept over to her, making sure to step lightly so my hooves didn't clack against the polished floor and give me away.

When I was a hair's width from her, I grabbed her waist. She shrieked, the pan clattering into the sink as I hoisted her into my arms.

"Alistair!" She squealed. "You scared the shit out of me!"

I sat her on the island and grinned. "Let me make it up to you."

Stepping into her space, I hooked my fingers into the waistband of her leggings and yanked them down her legs.

"What are you doing?" she gasped.

I lowered to my knees and threw her legs over my shoulders. "Brace yourself on your elbows, babe. It's time for dessert."

Gripping the backs of her thighs, I pulled her to the

edge of the counter, bringing that tasty little cunt right to my mouth.

"Alistair," she moaned at the first swipe of my tongue.

I groaned, running the wide pad of my tongue up and down her entrance, delighted by the fact that she was already wet and wanting.

"You taste so fucking good, Pam," I said between flicks of my tongue.

She whined and rolled her hips, driving my face into her cunt again.

"Grab my horns and ride my face," I mumbled.

Releasing one of her thighs, I held a hand out to her and pulled her up into a sitting position. The counter was probably freezing on her ass, but I didn't give a fuck. I wanted to taste her just like this.

Pam gripped my horns, and I dove between her thighs again. With each pass of my tongue over her clit, she rocked into me, gasping and mumbling unintelligible words under her breath.

I loved her like this, lost in her pleasure, allowing me to worship her pussy like she deserved.

I turned my attention to her entrance, pulsing my tongue in and out of her as fast as I could.

"Alistair," she breathed, thrusting against my face.

"That's it, sweetheart. Use me," I murmured against her center.

I ran one of my fingers alongside my tongue, getting it nice and wet before I brought it to her clit. With each swirl of my fingertips and each thrust of my tongue, her breathing increased, the clench of her thighs around my face getting tighter, and her heels digging into my back.

"Fuck, I'm gonna come," she rasped on the tail end of a moan.

Good.

I wanted her to come. Wanted her to leave my face fucking soaked.

Replacing my fingers with my tongue, I flicked the tip back and forth over her clit, and her hips bolted forward.

"Yes. Yes." She yanked my horns, pressing me so deep into her cunt that I could barely breathe.

I sucked her clit into my mouth, curling my lips around it and latching on hard, just how she liked it.

"Fuck! Alistair!" Her thighs clamped around my head, and she rode my face through her orgasm, her body spasming against me.

I worked her through it with slow strokes of my tongue, soothing away the hurt from how hard I'd sucked her clit.

Fuck.

My face was soaked, and my cock was throbbing.

I grazed my face along her inner thigh and groaned, "I gotta have you right now."

Before she could let go of my horns, I lifted her off of the counter, slammed the light switch, and carried her over to the fireplace.

Gently, I laid her down and carefully slid out from between her legs.

It only took a second before I was on top of her, caging her in with my arms and frantically pressing my lips to hers.

She wrapped her arms around my neck, threading her fingers through my hair and deepening the kiss. Our tongues clashed, our breaths coming out as desperate, labored pants.

My clothes and the hoodie covering her upper body felt like too much space between us. I wanted to be as close to her as possible.

"I need you," she groaned against my lips. "Please."

Her desperation made my cock throb.

My fingers found the hem of the hoodie, dragging it up her body. I broke the kiss and she tugged it over her head, exposing every inch of her bare skin.

My breath stuttered. Each beautiful curve of her body, from the softness of her stomach to the rounded slope of her breasts, was highlighted by the glow of the fire.

"Gods, you're stunning," I murmured.

She shook out her hair and set her glasses aside, looking up at me with a sensual smile while I admired her.

I tugged my shirt over my head in a rush, not giving a fuck about stretching the neckline. The moment I pulled my sweats and my underwear down, my cock sprang free, jutting up toward my stomach.

"Do you need lube?" I asked, giving my shaft a slow stroke.

I was more than happy to hoof it upstairs and grab it.

Propped up on her elbows and with her gaze locked with mine, she ran her fingers along her pussy. "Nope. Get over here and fuck me."

She didn't have to ask me twice.

I rushed between her parted legs, notching myself at her center and burying myself inside with a sharp thrust.

"Alistair," she groaned, arching her back and pushing her tits against my chest.

The stretch of her cunt around my cock made me shudder. From the tension in my balls, I could tell I wasn't going to last long.

"This tight cunt," I rasped. I ran my nose along the side of her face, puffing out a breath with another deep thrust. "I can't get enough of you, sweetheart."

Pulling out slightly, I slammed back in until my sheath rubbed against her sensitive clit. She threw her head back with a moan and I could already feel her walls gripping my cock.

I moved faster, bucking my hips so hard it jostled her body and bounced her tits against my chest.

Heat radiated off of the fire, making us slick with sweat. I dragged my tongue along her neck, savoring the salty taste of her skin. Her needy little moans, the slap of my balls, and my ragged grunts echoed through the room. It was heady and hypnotic, letting everything else slip away and losing myself in her.

She tightened her grip, the tips of her fingers digging into my back. "Fuck. Fuck. I'm gonna come."

I propped up on one arm, gripping her waist with the other to hold her in place.

I started to rut, pounding into her with harsh thrusts, my sheath dragging over her clit with each one.

"Alistair. Yes, yes." She closed her eyes and threw her head back, crying out as her orgasm tore through her.

Her pussy pulsed around me, tipping me over the edge. My spine tingled and my cock jerked inside her, filling her with spurt after spurt of cum.

She looked so beautiful panting underneath me with her greedy cunt milking my cock—but I wasn't done with her yet.

This was our last night together and I planned to make the most of it.

"Pam," I said her name on a heavy breath and pressed my damp forehead to hers. "I want you to ride me. Do you think your knees can handle that, sweetheart?"

She tensed and bit her lip. "I—That's another one of those things I don't have a lot of experience with."

"Hey." I wrapped a hand around the nape of her neck

and traced her jaw with my thumb. "If you don't want to try it, we don't have to. There are plenty of other ways I can—"

"No, I want to try."

I grinned down at her, admiring her willingness to try new things. "I'll help you then. I'll guide your hips and show you how to move. If it hurts or if you don't like it, we can stop."

Her expression softened and she smiled. "Alright."

"You stay put, I'm gonna grab some pillows for your knees."

Slowly, I pulled out, sneaking a glimpse of my cum dribbling out of her before standing up.

The couch was covered with throw pillows and I settled on two fluffy, down-filled squares. They'd provide a nice cushion between her knees and the carpet.

I laid with my horns pointing back toward the fireplace and put the pillows on either side of my hips.

Pam propped up on her elbows and looked over at me. "What about your cum? I don't want to get it on the rug."

I chuckled, because *fuck*, she was adorable. "It's just a little cum. I have a carpet cleaner. Now get over here and ride this cock like a good girl."

I'd just filled her with my cum, but I needed to feel her wrapped around my cock again.

She crawled over to me and I gave my cock a slow stroke at the sight of her. She was sweet and sexy, all my desires wrapped up into one perfect woman.

A perfect woman who was going to take a ride on my cock.

"Straddle me on all fours," I instructed.

She climbed overtop of me with her palms on the floor and her knees digging into the pillows. "Like this?"

Her breasts hung in front of me, the tips of her nipples caressing my chest.

"Just like that. I'm going to guide you onto my cock and then you can sit back."

She nodded and I gripped her hips, slowly guiding her entrance to the tip of my cock. I slid her on top of it and her breath hitched.

"Holy goddess," she gasped. I'd just fucked her and she was still so fucking tight.

"Good?" I asked with a smirk and she nodded.

I could feel the tip rubbing along her walls as her cum soaked cunt took every inch of my cock. Once I was buried up to my sheath, I eased my grip on her waist.

"Go ahead and sit back now, babe."

She leaned back on her knees, and I groaned, feeling her drag my cock along with her. I'd purposefully laid this way so the firelight radiated over her body. So I could see the bounce of her tits and the look on her face while she rode me.

I ran my hands up her thighs to the soft swell of her stomach. "Ready?"

"Yep." She nodded and I gripped her hips.

"I'll support you and you just move up and down, sweetheart." I lifted her hips and she moved with me, her cunt gliding along my shaft. "Yes, just like that," I groaned.

"This feels so good." She put her hands on top of mine and started to move faster.

"Look at you, my pretty little cowgirl. Fucking yourself on my cock."

I loved seeing her take control like this. To feel comfortable enough with me to try something new.

Increasing the pace, she rose up on her knees then came down on my cock, her ass rippling against my thighs. Cum spilled out of her with each thrust, trickling down her legs, onto my body, and the carpet beneath us.

Her lips parted with a soft moan and her hands drifted away from mine. One slid to her breast, cupping it a few times before rolling the nipple between her thumb and index finger. The other reached between her legs, massaging her clit to the rhythm of her body.

"Pam," I breathed, taking in the sight of her chasing her pleasure.

I forced my hips upward, meeting her thrust for thrust.

"Oh, fuck," she whined as our bodies collided. I could feel her cunt tightening around my cock and her thighs clamping my waist. "I'm going to come," she gasped. "Fuck. I'm going to come."

"Use me, beautiful," I grunted, forcing myself to hold out. "Come on my cock."

She moaned and drove me deep, rocking against me as her orgasm crashed into her.

"Gods yes," I rasped, tipping my head back to watch her ride me through my orgasm.

I dug my fingers into her waist, grinding against her and groaning at the pulse of her pussy around my cock. Warmth spread along my spine and my cock spasmed inside of her, filling her with cum until our bodies stilled.

"Shit," she breathed. Her body went slack and she leaned forward, resting her palms on my chest.

With my cock still buried inside of her, I wrapped my arms around her and rolled us onto our sides. Her damp bangs stuck to her forehead, and her chest heaved as she fought to catch her breath, but *fuck*, she was the most gorgeous thing I'd ever seen. I ran my fingers along the column of her neck and smiled.

"What?" she asked with a soft grin.

"I'm just thinking about how lucky I am to have a beautiful woman like you in my life."

She ran her hand along my chest, burying her fingers in the curls. "I'm lucky to have you."

I nuzzled her hair with my snout and kissed the top of her head. *Fuck, I was going to miss her*. "I wish you—"

"Shhh," she whispered. "Don't think about it. Just be in the moment with me."

TWENTY-THREE

PAM

"You are loved just for being who you are, just for existing"- Ram Dass

---

"Are you sure you don't want me to fly back with you?" Alistair asked pensively.

I adjusted Remi's bag on my shoulder and shook my head. "I'm sure."

I mean, I wanted him to fly back with me and never leave, but I couldn't ask that of him. It was a choice he had to make on his own.

He leaned over, bringing the rough portion of his horns that dipped down between his brows to my forehead. "I am going to miss you so much. Thank you again for doing this."

"I'll always be there for you when you need me."

He wrapped one hand around the back of my neck, his thumb gently tracing over my jawline. "Pam, I—"

Was he going to say what I thought he was going to say?

He couldn't possibly.

Could he?

Without another word, he pressed his mouth to mine, gently pushing his tongue past my lips. He tasted like sweet mint and strong coffee, his signature sage and cedar wrapping around me. My fingers tangled in the hair around the sides of his face, pulling him deeper, soaking up as much of him as I could right there in the middle of the airport.

He pulled away and shook his head, puffing out a breath. "Have a safe flight, okay? Text me as soon as you land."

"I will."

He squatted in front of me and rubbed a finger along the mesh of Remi's carrier. "Have a safe flight, buddy. I'll miss you."

I knew he would. He and Remi had a little bromance going.

Alistair stood and checked his watch. "You should probably head through security. Even with a first class ticket, you never know when they're going to hold you up."

I took a deep breath and nodded. "Alright."

He gave me one last kiss on the forehead and a strained lopsided smile. "Bye."

"Bye."

It felt like my feet were covered in cement as I walked away, every step weighed down by the pain of saying goodbye to Alistair.

I was positive he was staring at me. Just standing there watching me disappear into the sea of people waiting to go through security.

Tears pricked at the corners of my eyes, but I forced them back. I didn't want to draw extra attention to myself, and I'd have plenty of time to cry unnoticed on the plane ride back to Briar Glenn.

On the plane ride home.

I went through the motions with security, showing them my ID and waiting patiently while they ran the wand over Remi's carrier.

Luckily there wasn't much of a wait before it was time to board, meaning I had less time to stress about the flight. My medication made me feel nice and relaxed, but not as relaxed as I would have been if Alistair had been with me.

I sat down, taking deep breaths and running through the affirmations in my head.

I inhale peace and exhale worry.

I can do hard things.

I am calm and at peace.

Repeating them over and over, feeling my heart rate slow and the pre-flight jitters fading away.

A bell pinged in the lounge area. "Flight 363 to Briar Glenn is now boarding. The one p.m. flight to Briar Glenn is now boarding."

"That's us, buddy," I whispered to Remi, hoisting his carrier over my shoulder.

He responded with a desolate wail of discomfort, relaying exactly how he felt about being stuffed in his carrier again.

The flight attendant smiled wide and scanned my ticket. "Have a safe flight."

She was too chipper for the sadness I was feeling, but I forced myself to mumble thanks.

I walked down the jetway and through the door of the plane. A small smile curved up my lips at the memory of Alistair ducking his head to accommodate his horns while he passed through the low entrance.

I rushed to my seat, the tears threatening to fall and ruin my mascara.

Remi yowled with displeasure when I slipped him under the seat.

"I know, buddy," I reassured him. "We'll be home soon."

I fastened my seatbelt, and once the plane was boarded and the attendant had gone over the safety spiel, we moved down the runway.

This was what I'd come to dislike. The takeoff and landing.

The plane began to rumble, hopping off the runway as it picked up speed.

Shit.

I gripped the armrests, squeezing my eyes shut and gritting my teeth so hard my jaw hurt.

I inhale peace and exhale worry.

I can do hard things.

I am calm and at peace.

Maybe if I told myself enough times, I'd believe it. Just like I'd come to believe that I was worthy of romance—that I was worthy of love.

He was so close to saying it.

But maybe he didn't need to.

He showed me every day.

The weightless feeling of being in the air swept over me, and I loosened my grip on the armrest.

Peeking out the window, I watched as Colorado grew smaller until it disappeared beneath the cloud cover completely.

Just like that, he was gone.

Tears tracked down my cheeks, taking my mascara with them.

Whatever fantasy I'd been living in for the past week was over. I was leaving—and I was leaving a part of my heart behind.

"MOM!" Tegan jumped out of the car and wrapped me in a huge hug.

Alistair had offered to hire a car service, but Atlas and Tegan insisted on picking me up. I was positive it was because she wanted to grill me about the trip.

"Hey, Mom," Atlas said, kissing my cheek once Tegan finally released me. "Let me get those for you."

He easily picked up my suitcases and carried them around to the back of his truck.

Tegan climbed into the front seat, and I hoisted Remi and me into the back.

"How was your trip, Mom?" Tegan asked the second my seatbelt clicked.

"It was great. We had a great time."

I caught her staring at me in the rearview mirror. "Is everything okay? You look like you've been crying."

Atlas climbed into the truck, the door slamming behind him.

Saved by the son-in-law, or so I thought.

"Mom, is everything alright? Did something happen between you and Alistair?" she rushed out.

Atlas put on his seatbelt and merged into the airport traffic. "Baby, we talked about this," he said calmly.

She sighed, and I could practically hear her rolling her eyes. "I know we talked about this, but I don't want my mom to keep doing this if it hurts her."

I cleared my throat. "I'm a grown woman, and I'm capable of making my own decisions, thank you very much. I had an amazing time. It's just...hard to say goodbye."

"Did he decide what he's going to do with the company?" she asked, watching me in the rearview again.

I shook my head. "I didn't ask him what he's going to do."

"Mom," Tegan sighed. "What do you mean you didn't ask?"

"It isn't my place," I said with a shrug.

"You're his girlfriend. What do you mean it isn't your—" she started, but Atlas cut her off.

"Baby, I think what your mom is saying is that Alistair needs to make these sorts of decisions on his own. She doesn't want to influence him one way or the other. Right, Mom?"

I nodded. "It's a major life change. I don't want him to feel pressured. And even if he does sell his shares, I can't ask him to move to Briar Glenn. We've been dating for a little over a month. What if it doesn't work out, and he regrets it?"

"Do you remember what you told me, Mom? When Atlas and I started dating?"

As her mother, I gave her a lot of advice, but I didn't recall that conversation specifically.

From the corner of my eye, I caught Tegan slipping her hand over the center console, giving Atlas' hand a squeeze.

"You said that when the goddess brings two people together, she's never wrong. What's meant to be will be."

I shook my head, my mouth hanging open. "You remembered that?"

Tegan let out a little laugh. "How could I forget?" She turned around to look at me. "You've always believed in true love—at least for everyone else. What's stopping you from believing it for yourself?"

I realized now that I was worthy. I deserved the sort of love my kids had with their mates, the type of love in romance books and movies.

That was exactly what I had with Alistair.

TWENTY-FOUR

ALISTAIR

I choose to change my life one step at a time, and today I take that step.

My phone vibrated on the nightstand, and I rolled over, blindly reaching for it with my eyes half open.

It was a text message from Pam.

Pam: Good morning, loverboy.

Fuck. It was just the other day that she was in my bed, calling me that.

Me: Good morning, pretty lady.

I GROANED and stared at the empty pillow on her side of the bed. It was our first morning apart and I already hated waking up without her next to me.

How could I just let her go like that?

I was so close to telling her exactly how I felt about her.

Why did I stop myself?

Usually, I was so forward. But I didn't want to freak her out.

I mean, I'd known I was in love with her for a while now.

Hell, maybe even after our first date.

The conversation we'd had the night before she left changed things for me.

I'd spent so much of my life building companies and making money—but none of that mattered now. I wanted to spend the rest of my time with her.

I didn't want to waste a single second.

Standing with a groan, I stretched and opened my nightstand. Pulling out the little folded piece of paper with Jonathan's offer, I ran my fingers over the string of zeros that never seemed to end.

It was a lot of money—but I'd give it all up for her. Every single cent, I was sure of it.

That I'd get to walk away with it was just a perk.

I grabbed my phone—not giving a shit about what time it was—and called Jonathan.

He answered on the third ring.

"Al?" he asked in that 'just woke up' voice.

"Hey Jon, sorry to wake you—I wanted to get back to you about the offer. I accept. Have your lawyers draft a contract and send it to my lawyers."

"Really?" he asked, shocked and slightly more awake.

"Really. And, uh, you don't happen to know any good realtors, do you?"

"Lauren's cousin is one. I'll send you her info. And Al— thank you. For being my business partner and teaching me everything I know. I hope you enjoy your retirement."

I smiled, thinking of just how much Jonathan reminded me of myself. He'd take great care of the company. "Thank you, I plan to. Talk to you soon."

Before he could say anything else, I ended the call and let out a long exhale, feeling all the stress leave my body.

This wasn't the end.

This was the beginning of the rest of my life.

I found Chai's contact and hit 'call,' hoping she wasn't teaching a class.

"Hey Dad, what's up?"

"I accepted Jonathan's offer. I'm gonna sell the house and move to Briar Glenn," I blurted out in one rushed string of words.

Chai laughed. "It's about damn time. I was starting to wonder what was taking you so long. I knew you'd be done for once Pam went out there."

I grinned, shaking my head. "You know me better than I know myself."

"I mean, this stubbornness had to come from some-where." She was quiet for a second before finally asking, "Does Pam know?"

"Not yet. I, uh, I was hoping you could help me with something."

"Alright, Romeo. What do you have in mind?"

TWENTY-FIVE

PAM

Everything I trust comes to me exactly when I need it.

"Well, what did you think?" Chai asked as we walked out of our first hot yoga class.

Refusing to take no for an answer, she'd insisted I meet her in Rock Harbor to use the gift card from Alistair.

It was my second day back home and I didn't even get to hole up in the house and mope.

"If I'm being honest, it was like an hour-long hot flash." I wiped the sweat off my brow, and she laughed.

"If my dad asks, just tell him you loved it."

Her dad.

Every time I thought about Alistair, my chest felt tight.

We'd talked a few times—but he seemed more distant than usual. Like he was lost in his thoughts.

It made sense, considering he had some difficult decisions to make.

"Don't worry, I planned on it."

I'd hate to waste such an expensive gift, and maybe hot yoga would grow on me over time.

Chai dug through her bag and pulled out her phone. "Do you have any plans for the rest of the day?"

"A friend asked me to meet her for lunch, but I don't feel up to it—especially after that class. I'm just going to go home and relax."

Nancy was dying to hear more details about my trip, but she'd have to wait. I was physically and emotionally exhausted.

"Well," Chai said, her brows raised as she typed something on her phone. "I hope you can get some rest. I'll see you in class later this week?"

I nodded. "Wouldn't miss it. Oh, and if you talk to your dad, will you tell him to call me? He's been a little quiet. I just want to make sure he's okay."

She gave me a soft smile. "I'm sure you'll hear from him soon. Drive safe, okay?"

"You too, honey."

I hopped in my car, checking my phone for any texts or calls I might have missed before starting the engine.

Nothing.

It was still early. Maybe he was sleeping in. Or maybe he needed some distance while he processed things.

I wanted him to sell his shares and move here. I wanted to be able to see him without hopping on an airplane and flying halfway across the country.

I wanted to tell him that I was in love with him.

But it wasn't the right time.

I didn't want to be the reason he upended his life. I didn't want to influence his decision.

The 'Welcome to Briar Glenn' sign came into view, and

I pulled onto Main Street. While I loved visiting Colorado —and missed Alistair—I was happy to be home.

There was something special about this little town, and now that I'd traveled outside of it, I could finally appreciate it.

I turned onto my street, and right as I was about to pull into my driveway—I saw him.

Alistair Reid was sitting on my steps, his hands in his pockets and his face buried in the scarf I gave him.

My favorite scarf.

When he saw me, he flashed me that signature lopsided grin.

I couldn't park the car and hop out fast enough.

"What are you doing here?" I sputtered, rushing up the driveway toward him.

He shrugged—like it was such a casual thing that he was here. "Well, since I'm retiring, I thought I'd relocate to Briar Glenn. I was hoping you could help me find a place to stay."

Chai's words echoed in my head.

I'm sure you'll hear from him soon.

This was why she had been so insistent about the hot yoga class.

He opened his arms wide, wrapping me in a tight hug as tears welled up in my eyes.

"You accepted Jonathan's offer?"

"Mhmm," he mumbled against my hair. "The morning after you left, I called him first thing. Pam—" He wrapped his hand around the column of my neck, tilting my face to meet his gaze. "I should have told you this at the airport, but I'm in love with you. I love every single thing about you. The romance books, the mantras, the little snort you do when you laugh, the love you give to the people around you. I don't want to do the long-distance thing. I want to be *here*.

I don't want to waste a single second I could be spending with you."

I never thought I'd have something like this. Some surprise, impassioned declaration of love like you saw in movies and read about in romance books. Yet here I was, having my own *When Harry Met Sally* moment, standing with the man of my dreams while he professed his love for me.

And I knew he meant it.

"I love you, too." I ran my fingers through his curls and pressed my lips to his, my body fitting against his like we were two halves of the same whole.

It was one of those cinematic kisses where time stops, the background fades to a blur, and the only thing that matters at that moment is the two of you.

We'd found what our lives had been missing. This was our love story—and it was just the beginning.

EPILOGUE

ALISTAIR

> Pam: Are you on your way? Everyone is here waiting.

> Me: We just left. Chai couldn't decide on an outfit.

> Pam: See you soon 🩶

I sat my phone in my lap and ran my clammy hands over my thighs. I was nervous, and not because of Chai's driving.

We were on our way to Pam's for dinner, and I was meeting her family for the first time tonight.

Remembering Pam's favorite breathing technique, I took a deep breath, holding it in for three seconds before letting it out on a long exhale.

I inhale peace and exhale worry.

I inhale peace and exhale worry.

"Dad, will you relax," Chai said with a laugh. "I don't think I've ever seen you this worked up."

I tugged at the collar of my flannel shirt and cracked the window, letting some fresh air flow into the car. "I'm trying! I just want this to go smoothly. You and Pam get along so well. I want her kids to like me."

She laughed again and turned the car onto Pam's street. "Well, you don't have to worry about Tegan, and I'm sure Reece is going to like you. They just want their mom to be happy. Everything's going to be fine."

I looked over at her and smiled. "Thanks, kid."

"You know I've always got your back." She pulled into Pam's car-lined driveway. "This is it. Ready?"

I nodded. "Let's do this."

We walked up the front steps, and before I could knock on the door, it flew open.

"Hi!" Pam said, beaming at us.

She was dressed in a cream-colored turtleneck—one that I was positive she'd knit herself—and jeans, looking just as beautiful as she always did.

"Hi, pretty lady." I gave her a hug and a quick kiss. Being in her presence eased some of my anxiety, but there was still a knot in my stomach that wouldn't loosen up until the introductions were done.

"Come on in," Pam said, and we filed inside.

Remi greeted us, rubbing against my leg and holding his tail straight up.

"Hey, buddy." I crouched to pet him while Pam and Chai hugged.

We hung up our coats and followed Pam down the hallway. Immediately, I noticed that she'd put up a new photo. The one of me, her, and Remi in our matching sweaters. The one I'd taken when she came to visit me.

It was my phone background, but I stopped for a second to admire our smiling faces and the way we were effortlessly posed. You could practically feel the joy radiating from us. It would have been a small thing to most people, but I was honored to have earned a place on her wall.

"Everyone," Pam said when we stepped into the living room. "This is Alistair."

Pam's family was spread out on the couches, and all eyes snapped to me.

"Hi!" A carbon copy of Pam said and gave me an enthusiastic wave.

Tegan.

If I didn't know better, I would have assumed they were sisters.

She rushed over with Atlas in tow and wrapped me in a tight hug. "It's so nice to finally meet you."

"It's nice to meet you, too. Your mom has told me so much about you."

Atlas extended a giant paw and shook my hand in what could best be described as a death grip. "Nice to see you again, Mr. Reid."

"Please, call me Alistair," I said, flexing my hand to make sure my fingers were still intact.

His body swayed slightly with the slow wag of his tail. "I'll do my best."

They stepped aside, making space for Reece and his mate.

This was it.

I cleared my throat and extended a hand out to Reece. "It's wonderful to finally meet you."

He looked me up and down for a second with his mustache pursed over his lip before—he smiled?

I felt all the tension whoosh out of my body.

"Nice to meet you, Al," he said and gave my hand a strong shake. "My mom has told me so many wonderful things about you. I'm glad the family finally got the chance to meet you."

Well, that was a surprise.

He seemed delightful.

It was amazing what love and therapy could do.

His mate gave him a soft caress on the arm with his tentacle before extending a webbed hand to me. "Lovely to meet you, Alistair. I'm Cyrus, Reece's mate."

A seven-hundred-year-old kraken with a British accent.

Now *that* was something you'd read about in a romance novel.

I shook his hand, watching as his tentacle clenched his arm. "It's great to meet you, Cyrus. Pam mentioned that you're a vinyl aficionado too."

He nodded enthusiastically. "Yes, you'll have to come over sometime and check out my collection."

"I'd love that."

Reece shoved his hands in his pockets and cleared his throat. "My mom tells me you're quite the outdoorsman, Al. I think you'll love it here in Briar Glenn. Plenty of parks and trails. Maybe all of us can get out for a hike once the weather warms up."

I was dumbfounded.

Reece Rollins—my girlfriend's supposedly grumpy son—had just invited me to go hiking.

"That would be great."

Reece gave me a little nod of his head, and the two of them went to join Atlas and Tegan.

Chai sidled up beside me and whispered. "See, that wasn't so bad, now was it?"

"It went a lot better than I expected it to go."

"They know Pam loves you, Dad. And you know what? In time, they'll love you, too. How could they not?"

She was going to make me cry.

"Come here, kid." I hugged her tightly and kissed the top of her head.

"Dad, you're embarrassing me in front of my boss," she hissed under her breath.

"Don't care," I said, squeezing her one more time before letting her go.

"Alright," Pam said, clapping her hands together. "Now that everyone's met, I think it's time to eat."

All the kids filed toward the dining room, leaving Pam and me behind.

She put her hands on my waist and gazed up at me. "I told you everything was going to be fine."

I leaned over and wrapped my hand around the nape of her neck, pulling her close. "You did."

"I love you," she whispered, staring into my eyes.

"I love you too."

I pressed my lips to hers, kissing her once everyone was out of the room—like we were just a couple of kids.

APRIL

PAM

I am fulfilled.
I deserve the love I receive.
I am grateful for the people who love me.

I let out a deep breath and opened my eyes, thankful it was finally warm enough in Briar Glenn to take my yoga practice outside. A spring breeze whipped by, showering me with a flurry of cherry blossoms and sending a chill down my spine.

Maybe I was getting ahead of myself with the warm enough stuff.

Alistair burst through the door of his RV, drawing my attention.

"Got you some coffee, sweetheart," he said, carefully walking over with two steaming mugs in his hands.

"Thank you, babe." I grabbed the mug and took a sip.

Just how I liked it.

Gods, he was the man of my dreams.

He sat on his mat with a groan, taking a sip of his coffee as more cherry blossoms rained down on us.

"I can't believe I get to call this place home." Tilting his head back, his curls blowing in the breeze, he grinned.

"Better than Colorado?" I asked, admiring how handsome he looked.

He set his cup down and looked over at me. "Of course it's better than Colorado. You're here."

I felt my cheeks growing hot.

Months later and I was still swooning over him.

Speaking of swooning.

"Tell me again how you got those Alanis tickets." I raised my brows and took another sip of my coffee.

He chuckled. "I told you, I know a guy who knows an orc."

"Alistair Reid, I swear if you paid an arm and a leg for those tickets—"

"Shhh. A concert is on the list. We have to do it."

The list of all the things I'd never done that we were slowly working our way through.

We sat there for a second, listening to the rustle of the trees swaying in the breeze, before Alistair finally spoke.

"Hey," he asked slyly. "Reece dropped off my uniform the other day. Do you want to see it?"

Not one to retire full-time, Alistair had applied for the Park Ranger position at the Briar Glenn Campground. As the head of the Briar Glenn Parks and Recreation Department, Reece was more than happy to give him the position —after a warning about the Moth Madam, that is.

The position allowed Al to live on-site in his RV, but when the campground closed for the winter, I was hopeful he'd move in with me and Remi.

"Yeah, why don't you go put it on?"

He bit his lip. "I, uh, I didn't mean like that. I was thinking maybe we could do a little role-play. Act out that

scene we read the other day. Maybe play with our new toy."
He leaned over, his whiskers tickling my ear. "Would you
like that? I know how much you love being my good girl."

I set my cup down and raced him to the RV, the two of
us practically climbing over one another to get through the
door.

Yes, book boyfriends exist.

And I found mine in Alistair Reid.

BUT ASHLEY

Did they ever use the steam room?
Sign up at the link in my Instagram bio to find out!
@ashleybennettauthor

ACKNOWLEDGMENTS

A special thank you to:

Conky- Thank you for bringing Pam and Alistair to life. As always, I'm lucky to work with you, but even luckier to call you a friend.

Clio and Beatrix- Thank you for always supporting me, reading for me, and just being two of the best friends I could ask for. You help me stay sane.

Rae- My wonderful PA. Thank you for all that you do for me and for being a great friend.

Kassie- We can do hard things.

Maggie- You are a gem. Can't wait to meet you in Colorado!

Anne-Marie, Ahren, Jen, Torri, Stephanie- Thank you for all of your feedback and for hyping me up! I appreciate all of you so much!

Remi and Christine- Thank you for sensitivity reading!

An anonymous author friend- Thank you for letting me pick your brain about menopause and for being an all around amazing person.

Wendy- Thank you for embracing my chaos and editing this book!

The Beignets- All of you lift me up on a daily basis, and I wouldn't be nearly as confident without your support. Thank you for everything!

ABOUT THE AUTHOR

Ashley Bennett

Ashley loves to write spicy-sweet monster romances. You can expect fluffy vibes and all the feels from her characters and stories. She enjoys brown sugar oatmilk iced lattes, stockpiling candles, the perfection of fall weather, thrifting mid-century modern furniture, and a good nonhuman romance. **She also loves to commission NSFW art.**

If you're interested in learning more about her upcoming projects or receiving special content, sign up for her newsletter here.

Connect with Ashley here.
    Purchase signed copies here!
    For access to exclusive content and merchandise, join me on Patreon.

ALSO BY ASHLEY BENNETT

The Leviathan Fitness Series

Made in United States
Troutdale, OR
03/02/2024

18147915R00146